"I still think it's a dangerous game."

"But you'd play it…if I asked you to?"

He didn't answer her for a moment.

"Nick?" She frowned.

"Yes…I said I'd do it. But don't say I haven't warned you." Nick reached out a hand and tipped her chin up so that he could look into her eyes. "Toying with people's emotions is always dangerous. You need to forget Stephen Harrington ever existed."

"I don't need you to tell me what to do, Nick." Kate glared at him. "And I am forgetting about Stephen."

"If you were forgetting about him you wouldn't be wasting your time trying to think of ways to make him jealous."

"If you're referring to my going to the wedding with you, you can forget about it. It was a passing thought and not a very good one. No one would believe we were lovers anyway."

"Wouldn't they?" Nick's voice was dangerously low. "Are you trying to issue some kind of a challenge?"

DO NOT
Disturb

Anything can happen behind closed doors!

Do you dare find out…?

Welcome again to DO NOT DISTURB!

Pretending to be Kate's escort at a wedding proves to be surprisingly easy for Nick—too easy, in fact—and as night falls their luxuriously sensual hotel suite is irresistibly inviting. But what will happen when the cold light of day follows the fiery heat of the moment?

Find out if Nick and Kate have finally found what they've both been looking for, in this sizzling tale of passion and seduction from much-loved Presents® author Kathryn Ross!

Kathryn Ross

THE NIGHT OF THE WEDDING

DO NOT *Disturb*

HARLEQUIN®

TORONTO • NEW YORK • LONDON
AMSTERDAM • PARIS • SYDNEY • HAMBURG
STOCKHOLM • ATHENS • TOKYO • MILAN • MADRID
PRAGUE • WARSAW • BUDAPEST • AUCKLAND

ISBN 0-373-12276-4

THE NIGHT OF THE WEDDING

First North American Publication 2002.

CHAPTER ONE

Was Stephen going to propose to her tonight? Kate wondered as she cycled home from work. The idea came into her head from nowhere and with it came a feeling of nervous anticipation, but surprisingly not the burst of joy she would have expected.

Why didn't the thought make her happy? They had been living together for two years now and they had agreed that if everything worked out they'd get engaged on their second anniversary. Things were working out, weren't they? Suddenly she wasn't sure.

Then she felt impatient with herself. Of course things were working out. Stephen was happy in his job now, and her job at the small publishing house of Temple and Tanner was challenging and exciting. And they both loved living in this city.

Amsterdam was bathed in beauty. The tall, majestic buildings glowed in the evening summer sun, their reflections shimmering in the waters of the canal. Pavement cafés were coming to life, buzzing with the low hum of conversation as friends met up after work, just as she was on her way to meet up with her best friend Nick Fielding again. The thought caused a frisson of pleasure to surge through her body as she hurried towards the last bridge and the café where they usually met for a drink after work.

It was five weeks since she had last seen Nick because he had been back in London on business. She had missed him, missed his sound advice, his infectious laugh. He always made her feel good.

Nick saw her immediately as she rode over the bridge, her long dark hair streaming back from her face. She wore a grey pair of trousers with a pretty pink strappy top that showed the perfection of her supple figure. As usual she was cycling one-handed and far too fast, with a large heavy rucksack on her back.

He watched as she hopped off the bicycle and chained it to the railings. Then she turned and saw him and waved, a smile lighting the beauty of her heart-shaped face.

She was thirty-two, only a year younger than him, but she looked about seventeen. Really she had changed very little since their days together at college, he thought as he watched her make her way through the crowded tables towards him.

'Hi, Katy.' Nick stood up as she approached the table and reached to kiss her on the cheek. Her skin was soft and smooth. She smelt sweetly of summer. Honeysuckle... or was it roses?

'You've changed your perfume,' he remarked as he pulled back from her, thinking with a pang about the bottle of her usual scent that he had purchased at the airport for her next birthday.

'Yes, Stephen bought it for me ages ago and I thought I'd better use it up before it went off.' Kate took off her rucksack and sat down opposite him. 'So how are you?' she asked with a smile.

She looked fabulous; her skin glowed with health, her wide green eyes sparkled with devilment. 'I'm fine—' he sat back down and put up a hand to catch the waitress's attention '—but I'm glad to be back. The London office was in chaos. I spent the first week just getting the files in order.'

She laughed. 'I bet they heaved a sigh of relief when you left. You're such a perfectionist, Nick.'

'When you run your own business you've got to be.'

The waitress came over and he ordered two coffees.

Kate suddenly noticed the woman at the next table was staring at him, open admiration in her eyes. Nick was extremely handsome, she agreed as she looked back at him. He had a fabulous physique, and he looked every inch the successful businessman that he was. The cut of his clothes was stylish, the light-coloured jacket and open-necked shirt emphasized his dark, almost Latin good looks. She felt a sudden dart of pride that he was her friend. Women had come and gone in his life, but their relationship remained constant, never changing. No matter how long it was since they had seen each other, there was always this easiness between them.

'I hope you didn't spend all of your time in London working on your computers,' she said as the waitress left them. 'You were supposed to be taking time out to show Serena the sights, weren't you?'

He shrugged ruefully. 'Things didn't quite work out.'

Something in his tone of voice made her frown. 'What do you mean?'

'I mean that our relationship has reached an end,' he said bluntly.

'Oh, Nick!' Kate leaned back in her chair. Although she was surprised at the suddenness of the break-up, she couldn't honestly say she was shocked. She had always known deep down that Serena wouldn't get Nick. 'I'm so sorry.'

He shrugged. 'Just one of those things,' he said easily.

She met the darkness of his eyes. 'Did you finish with her?' she asked softly.

'It was a mutual thing,' he murmured evasively, but Kate didn't believe a word of it. Serena was a beautiful leggy blonde but, despite her gorgeous looks and pleasant personality, Kate had always suspected that Serena was more serious about Nick than he was about her.

'So, what happened? Serena seemed so happy before you left. She was really looking forward to you showing her around London.'

'We had a nice time and we've parted on good terms.' Nick said nonchalantly, 'but we both wanted different things out of the relationship.'

The waitress brought their coffee as Kate digested this information. She presumed he meant Serena had wanted the relationship to deepen and he hadn't. Kate had seen it all before. Any time one of Nick's girlfriends started to move too close to him, or even hint around the possibility that the relationship might get serious, that was his cue to start to back away.

'It's a shame,' she murmured. 'I really liked Serena.'

'So did I,' Nick agreed easily.

'But not enough.'

Nick didn't answer that. 'We had been going out together for quite a while. I think we both agreed it was time to move on—'

'You had been going out together for five months,' Kate cut across him dryly. 'But, come to think about it, maybe you're right, maybe that is a long time for you, Nick.'

He met her eyes across the table, and then smiled. 'I didn't know I had been dating her for five months. Have you been keeping count?'

'No.' She frowned. 'I just remember, that's all… women do remember those kind of details.'

'Do they?' He drank his coffee. 'I don't think Serena was counting.'

'Anyway,' she cut across him, warming to her theme, 'apart from Jayne, all your relationships in these last few years haven't lasted long. In fact, I think Serena might hold the record after Jayne.'

'You think I'm on the rebound from Jayne?' he asked calmly.

'No.' She frowned. That thought hadn't really crossed her mind. His relationship with Jayne had ended over two years ago, and, although he'd been sad that they'd parted, Kate had always assumed that he had been the one to initiate the break-up. 'No…I suppose what I'm saying is that I'm starting to think you've got a problem with commitment.'

Nick grinned. 'Is that a bad thing?'

Kate looked at him askance. 'You've got to settle down at some point in time.'

'Why?'

'Well… Don't you want to have a family?'

'Not particularly. In fact I'm starting to think that variety is the spice of life.' His grin stretched even wider at the look on her face.

'You don't mean that, do you?'

'Not really.' He finished his coffee. 'But I'd rather be on my own than with the wrong person.'

'I agree with you there.' For a moment Kate was silent, her green eyes serious. Is Stephen the right person for me? she wondered. Then was appalled that she had asked herself that question. OK, Stephen had been a bit edgy recently, and there'd been an atmosphere between them that had never been there before. But he was probably tense because he was thinking about proposing to her, worrying about making the final commitment. The more she thought about it, the more likely that seemed. When he'd asked this morning what time she would be home from work, maybe he'd been planning ahead booking a table at an intimate little restaurant. That was why there had been that serious tone in his voice. She smiled at the thought. Everything would be fine. 'I'd like to have children, one day,' she said thoughtfully.

'You've got plenty of time for all that.' Nick's voice was dismissive.

'Have I?' She frowned. 'I've been so wrapped up in my career that everything else has been pushed on a back burner. But I would like a family one day, and that's something I can't keep putting off.'

'When it's the right time you'll know and it will happen.'

Maybe that was how it would be if Stephen proposed. When he actually said the words, maybe these sudden doubts would disappear, and she'd know he was the right person and this was the right time. She was accusing Nick of being scared of commitment, but maybe she was too.

'You've always been a bit of a fatalist, haven't you, Nick?' Kate smiled. 'I suppose I am as well. For instance, I do believe that there is someone for everyone…our ideal partner is out there waiting.'

Nick shook his head and laughed. 'That's not being a fatalist, Katy, it's being romantic.'

'There are such things as soul mates,' Kate maintained firmly. 'I mean, look at your mum and dad. They are still really happy and still very much in love even after all these years.'

'Yes, they are,' Nick agreed.

'Did you make time to go and see them when you were in London?'

He nodded. 'They both send you their love.'

Kate smiled. She really liked Nick's family. He had an older brother and a younger sister; all were lovely, friendly, caring people. She wished she had grown up in such a warm and secure environment. Kate had been an only child and her parents had divorced when she was ten. Her father had never had any time for her, and although her mother had tried to make up for this, she had had to work long hours just to keep the home together. In consequence, Kate had spent a lot of time round at Nick's house. His sister Rachael had been in her class and they had all been good friends. Rachael was in Australia now, happily married with two children.

'How are things with you and Stephen?' Nick asked.

'OK.' She smiled even more brightly at him.

Something about the way she said the word, the way she met his eyes, made alarm bells ring inside Nick. He frowned. 'You've got something to tell me, haven't you?'

She paused for a second, and then pursed her lips in a soft pout. 'It's our anniversary today, two years since we moved in together.'

'Congratulations.'

'Thanks.' She sighed. 'I can't believe it is two years, it seems to have flown.'

'And…?' He watched her quizzically.

'Crikey! I can't keep anything from you, can I?' She shook her head. 'There really isn't anything to tell.'

'Yes, there is. I can tell by the look in your eyes.'

'I shouldn't say anything because I'm not really sure,' she said hesitantly. 'But I have a feeling Stephen might propose to me tonight.'

There was a moment's silence. A moment when Kate suddenly realized how important his response to that news was to her.

'You think Stephen is going to propose marriage to you?' Nick looked totally shocked.

'No, I think he's probably going to propose that I become his business manager,' Kate drawled sardonically. 'Of course marriage—why are you looking at me like that? Is it really so hard to believe that Stephen would want to commit to me?'

'No…of course not.' Nick shook his head. 'It's just… I didn't think you two were getting on so well lately.'

'What made you think that?'

'I don't know. Maybe it was my imagination.'

'Well, everything is fine between us.' Kate swallowed hard and tried to ignore the ominous feelings inside her. Was everything all right between them? Would she be making a terrible mistake if she said yes to Stephen?

'If he does ask, will you be pleased for me?' Suddenly she was seeking reassurance. Her eyes held with the intense darkness of his, she felt as if she was holding her breath.

'If it's what you want,' Nick said steadily, coolly. 'Of course I would be pleased for you. I want you to be happy, Katy, you deserve to be happy.'

'Thanks.' She smiled at him, but at best it was a tremulous smile. Something was wrong, something was terribly wrong, but she couldn't figure out what it was. Cycling here, she had felt a moment's disquiet…but that was nothing to the weight of foreboding pressing on her now, and she couldn't place where it was coming from.

She tried to picture Stephen in her mind as he proposed to her, a faintly nervous, anxious look in his blue eyes, his hair flopping down on his forehead in that Hugh Grant way. 'Stephen is right for me.' She smiled at Nick. 'Oh…I know you think he's a bit irresponsible and I suppose he is sometimes…but he loves me and he's kind and he's funny and—'

'Why are you working so hard to convince me, Katy?' Nick cut across her quietly.

'I'm not!' Kate frowned. 'I'm just saying that I think

this is the right thing for me. I'm ready to make the commitment.'

'Well, I'm pleased for you.'

There was an edge to Nick's voice, an expression in his eyes that she couldn't fathom. She frowned again. 'I shouldn't have told you today.'

'Why?'

'Because you've just finished with Serena and you're obviously not in the best of moods.'

Nick shook his head. 'I'm fine, Katy,' he said gently. 'And I'm really happy for you.'

'Really?'

He nodded and reached to take her hand across the table. 'He's a lucky guy.'

Kate looked down at his hand against hers. The touch of his skin made her heart thump peculiarly. She felt odd, as if she had been running somewhere and had suddenly lost her sense of direction.

Nick took his hand away and looked at his watch. 'Well, I guess we'd better get going. You've got a big night ahead of you, and I've got work to do.'

'You work too hard,' she murmured. 'You need to cut down on the time you spend in front of those computers, find a nice girl and settle down.'

'I don't think that's very likely. I'm just bachelor material.' Nick grinned and shook his head. 'And you sound like my mother—'

'A very wise woman,' Kate inserted promptly. She felt a bit better again, as if whatever had been wrong had passed like an eclipse of the sun and things were back to normal.

Nick caught the waitress's eye to indicate he wanted to pay her. 'I'll get this,' he said as Kate reached to open her bag.

'Thanks. I'll get it next time.' They both stood up and walked together around the tables to the edge of the pavement.

'Have a good evening.' He bent to kiss her on the cheek. Although she was tall, almost five seven, Nick always made her feel petite; she wondered how tall he actually was—six feet four, she'd say at a guess.

'I'll ring you tomorrow and tell you all.'

He grinned at her. 'Maybe you'd better spare my blushes.'

She smiled.

'See you later, Kate.'

'Yes, see you later.' She turned away as he walked towards his open-topped Mercedes sports car. She unlocked her bicycle and put her bag over her shoulder. Before turning to go home, she noticed the woman who had been sitting at the next table to them was walking towards Nick. She smiled at him and said something and he stopped.

Would Nick ever get married? Kate wondered as she rode away. She supposed one day, despite all his protestations, a woman would sweep him off his feet, and he would have eyes for nobody but her. The thought settled around her like a dull cloud. He'd still have time for his friends, of course, she told herself swiftly. And anyway, it would probably be years before he decided to tie the knot; she could be old and grey with four children before Nick decided to walk down the aisle. Men could afford to take their time; they didn't have a biological clock ticking inside them.

She looked at her watch as she rode slowly down by the side of the canal. She was nearly an hour early. She'd told Stephen that she'd be home by seven-thirty. Usually she had a couple of coffees with Nick, and as she hadn't seen him for so long she had thought today that they would spend at least an hour chatting and catching up on news from London. But maybe it was just as well that she was going home early—as Nick had said, she had a big evening ahead. This way she'd have plenty of time to do her hair and get changed before Stephen got in from work.

What should she wear? She didn't want to appear too dressed-up—she'd look a fool if he hadn't really booked a restaurant and suggested getting a take-away. And maybe he wouldn't propose to her at all.

There was almost a feeling of relief inside her at that thought. Perhaps she needed a bit more time to get used to the idea. Moving in together had been a big enough step for her…marriage seemed an enormous leap into the abyss.

Certainly Nick hadn't seemed overly pleased for her. But then, for some reason Nick had never really warmed to Stephen. Not that he had ever said anything detrimental, and the two men were always perfectly civil to each other, but Kate had always known that Nick had reservations about him.

You couldn't be friends for as many years as they had, through school and college, and not learn to read the signs. She could tell by the sardonic gleam that lit the darkness of Nick's eyes sometimes, and the smile that wasn't quite so easy or relaxed when Stephen was around. Her partner was not someone Nick would have chosen for her, but it was only because he worried about her, and Stephen was so totally opposite to him in every way.

Nick took his career and his business running a computer firm very seriously. For Stephen, work was just a means to an end…he had changed jobs three times in the last year. He was wild about heavy rock music and in his spare time played in a band. Life was a bit of a roller-coaster ride with Stephen, but Kate had to admit it was exciting.

She slowed down even more as their apartment came into sight. It was on the ground floor of a very impressive patrician eighteenth-century mansion that overlooked the canal. The rent was astronomical and perhaps a bit more than they could really afford, but Kate had fallen in love with the place on sight and had decided she'd rather cut down on a few luxuries and live there than anywhere else.

She noticed the light in the front salon was on. Stephen was home early as well. She locked her bike against the front railings and ran up the steps to the door and let herself in.

The door closed with a bang behind her; her footsteps echoed on the polished wooden floor. 'Stephen,' she called out as she walked into the salon.

Even though it wasn't dark outside all the side lamps were on and the main chandelier blazed over the antique furniture. She flicked a couple of the lamps off as she passed towards the kitchen. There was a bottle of champagne cooling in a bucket on the table and two champagne glasses sat out waiting. But there was no sign of Stephen.

'Stephen honey, where are you?' Kate walked back through to the hallway. Then heard music coming from the bedroom. It wasn't the usual heavy rock that Stephen liked to listen to; this was softer, more romantic.

She paused with her hand on the bedroom door. There was a strange noise coming from the room, like someone gasping for air.

Kate pushed open the door.

Stephen sat up in bed and stared at her in horror.

'Stephen...?' In a kind of blank disbelief she stared back at him and then at the woman who lay beside him.

Shock unlike anything she had ever experienced before lashed through her.

'Oh, hell!' Stephen raked a hand through his blond hair, an apologetic, nervous look on his handsome features.

'Sorry, Kate.'

CHAPTER TWO

KATE sat alone in the apartment in total shock for hours watching the light fade.

The earlier scene played and replayed in her head with mind-blowing clarity. The woman—'Natasha,' Stephen had called her—had got up, dived into a T-shirt and a pair of jeans and disappeared into the bathroom.

'She's a colleague from work,' Stephen murmured as he reached for his clothes.

His calmness had brought fury rushing through her veins. A thousand questions fought for position, but all she'd said was, 'You'd better get out.' her voice trembling with rage.

'Out?' He had looked stunned. Like a little boy who had been told that Christmas had been cancelled. 'Out where?'

'Out of the apartment…out of my life.'

'Oh, come on, Kate…we need to talk things over—'

'I think the time for talking is over.'

She had watched from the front windows as they'd left. Stephen had put a small case and his guitar in the back of a red sports car. The woman's wheat-blonde hair had swung jauntily as she'd got behind the wheel. Then they'd roared off.

She was glad she hadn't cried—at least she had kept her dignity. She was glad she had restrained her temper as well. Neither of those emotions would have served her well, and at least that woman hadn't got the satisfaction of seeing her break.

But now, alone and desolate, Kate felt the tears welling up inside her. She swallowed them down, fiercely. Then on impulse she stood up, picked up her bag and left the apartment.

As she cycled along the road, the fairy lights on the bridges twinkled softly in the dusky purple of the evening. Lovers strolled hand in hand towards a brightly lit restaurant. It was a place Stephen had often taken her to. She had imagined he might take her there tonight. How could she have been so stupid? she wondered. She felt numb inside, as if all of this were unreal, some kind of sick dream.

She cut down a side street, the breeze whipping through her hair, cooling the fierce heat of her skin.

She didn't know where she was going until she turned down Nick's road. It was as if she were operating by remote control.

Nick lived in a converted warehouse. His offices were one side, his apartment the other. Kate pressed the front doorbell a couple of times but there was no answer. Where was he? she wondered. Maybe that woman from the café had detained him; perhaps they were out having a drink together.

Relief flooded through her as she heard footsteps and the door swung open, bathing her in warm, mellow light.

Nick had changed out of his suit and was wearing a pair of blue chinos and a blue shirt. He looked relaxed, and handsome. Kate felt her heart twist painfully. She had never felt so glad to see him.

'I was starting to think you were out,' she said with a wobbly smile.

'And I thought you'd be on champagne in some fabulous restaurant by now, an enormous diamond ring on your finger.' He stepped back so that she could come inside. 'What's happened?' He closed the front door, his eyes flicking over her, taking in the fact that she was wearing the same clothes as earlier, then locking on the extreme pallor of her skin.

'Katy, what's wrong?'

'Stephen has been having an affair.' She kept her voice steady with extreme difficulty. 'I caught him with her…in our bed.'

She didn't know what happened, but one moment she was standing there, telling him in what she thought was an incredibly brave voice, and the next she was in his arms and he was cradling her close, hushing her as she broke down into sobs.

'It'll be OK,' he murmured gently, stroking her hair back from her face. 'You'll get through this.'

'No, I won't,' she sobbed. 'How could he do this to me, Nick? I thought when we moved in together that we were making a commitment; it was such a big step for me. He talked me into it, for heaven's sake! Told me that he looked on it as a prelude to us getting married. I thought we were a couple, that we would be faithful and…God, I've been such an idiot.'

'No, you haven't.'

'I didn't have a clue, not one clue that he was seeing someone else.' Kate closed her eyes and shuddered. 'Talk about naïve…you must think I'm really stupid. All that talk about him proposing to me and all the time…'

'I don't think you're stupid. I think you are a very intelligent and lovely woman,' Nick said softly.

'You're just being kind,' she murmured.

'No, I'm not.' He pulled back from her and regretfully she broke away from his embrace. She had wanted to stay in his arms for a bit longer. She liked the feel of his body, warm and masculine against hers; it made her feel protected, cherished.

He tipped her face up towards his and studied her for a moment, his hand resting against her chin. Her heart seemed to give a very strange tilt as he wiped away the remains of the tears from her cheek with a gentle brush of his fingertips. 'He's not worth your tears, Katy,' he said softly.

'Probably not.' Her voice trembled, but strangely she wasn't thinking about Stephen now, she was thinking about the touch of Nick's hand against her skin. There was something sensual about the caress, something disturbingly sexy in the husky male undertone of his voice.

Kate frowned. What the hell was the matter with her? she wondered. She must be so upset by Stephen that she was imagining things.

He turned away from her and led the way through to the lounge. 'I'll fix you a drink,' he said.

'Thanks.' Her eyes flicked over the familiar room. It was comfortable, ultra-modern in design with a masculine stylishness, no ornaments, just plain blue settees against the wooden floor, and a few coloured rugs, no curtains on the window, just plain wooden blinds that he never drew down.

He had a workstation at the far end of the enormous room; a lamp was trained on it, spotlighting the computer that was turned on.

'I'm sorry, I've interrupted your work,' she murmured.

'You haven't interrupted anything.' Nick stood with his back to her as he poured their drinks. She noticed how wide his shoulders were, how narrow his hips. He has the body of an athlete, she thought idly.

'I'm glad you've come over. That's what friends are for, isn't it?' He turned and walked over to hand her a glass of brandy. 'What is it they say—a trouble shared is a trouble halved?'

She smiled wanly. 'I'm sure you could do without my problems.' She looked at the glass. Kate didn't usually drink spirits; a glass of wine on odd occasions was about as much as she imbibed.

'Brandy is good for shock,' Nick said. 'Just take a few sips.'

She nodded and sat down on the settee.

'I just can't believe he's done this to me, Nick.' She stared at the amber liquid in the balloon glass. 'He told me he loved me.'

There was silence between them for a moment. Nick sat down on the settee opposite her. 'Where is he now?'

'I told him to go and he did.'

'With the woman?'

Kate nodded.

'Who is she?'

'I'd never seen her before.' She shrugged. 'He said she was a colleague from work. Her name is Natasha; she's blonde and cute. Probably about nineteen.'

'Maybe you should just be grateful that you've found out now...he could have strung you along for ages—'

'Maybe he *has* been stringing me along for ages,' Kate muttered, swirling the drink around the glass. 'Maybe he never really loved me at all.' She looked up at Nick sharply. 'Did you know?'

'Know what?'

'That Stephen was cheating on me. Is that why you looked so shocked when I told you I thought he was going to propose?'

Nick shook his head. 'I had no idea. If I had, I'd have told you.'

'Would you?'

'Of course I would. I care about you too much not to have said something.'

Kate took a sip of her drink, feeling it warm her deep inside. 'Have you eaten?' Nick asked her.

She shook her head. 'I'm not hungry.'

'I'll make you something. I've got steak in the fridge.'

'Thanks, Nick, but honestly I couldn't eat anything. I should be going anyway.' She glanced at her watch and was surprised to see it was nearing midnight. 'I didn't realize it was so late, you've got work tomorrow and so have I,' she murmured, swallowing the rest of her drink. 'I'd better go.'

'You don't have to,' he said quietly.

She looked over at him.

'The spare room is made up,' he said.

Kate hesitated; the thought of her empty apartment was not welcoming. Plus she would have to completely strip the bed. She raked a hand through her hair, feeling suddenly sick.

'I haven't brought any night things.' She shook her head. 'I should go home.'

'I'll lend you a T-shirt and I've got a new toothbrush in the cupboard.' Nick grinned at her, a teasing light in his dark eyes. 'Now, how can you possibly turn down an offer like that? You're very honoured, you know. I don't hand out T-shirts and toothbrushes to just anybody.'

She smiled.

'That's better.' He suddenly became serious. 'Don't go home to that apartment tonight, Katy.'

'I must admit, I don't want to go back there,' she admitted huskily.

'Well, that's settled, then.' He stood up. 'Come on, I'll show you up to your room.'

It felt strange following Nick upstairs to the bedrooms.

Although she had been to his home on many occasions, she had never stayed overnight and had only seen upstairs once when he had first moved in.

For some reason there was a feeling of awkwardness inside her as he opened the door into the spare room. Why, she couldn't have said, but the sight of the enormous double bed was somehow provocative enough to make her feel self-conscious. Maybe it was just the way she was feeling at the moment. She was edgy and tense, and no wonder after the shock of seeing Stephen with someone else.

She tried to turn her thoughts to the décor; the plain Shaker-style furniture and the pictures on the wall made it a very sophisticated and relaxing room.

'There's an *en suite* bathroom through here.' Nick opened a door into a luxurious bathroom, flicking on all the lights.

'This is really very kind of you, Nick,' Kate murmured hesitantly as he turned back into the bedroom and she found herself standing very close to him.

'You'd do the same for me…wouldn't you?' he asked with a grin.

'Well, I would if I had a spare room,' she said, trying to lighten the tension inside her and smile at him.

'That's OK, then.' His eyes moved over her face, and lingered for a second on her lips.

She felt her throat tighten, her breathing restrict. She wondered suddenly what it would be like to be kissed by Nick, to be held properly in his arms, not just to be comforted, but caressed. He would probably be a fabulous lover. How could he be otherwise? He was so incredibly sexy and yet so tender. Her heart missed a couple of beats. Then she looked away from him, shocked by her thoughts.

'I'll go and get you that T-shirt.'

As he disappeared out of the room, Kate sat down on the side of the bed. Her heart was thumping as if she had been running in a race. She felt ashamed of herself for thinking such thoughts—if Nick knew what she had been thinking, he would probably be horrified. He thought of her as a sister.

Her reflection stared back at her from the dressing table opposite. She looked awful: her skin was ashen, her eyes swollen from her tears, her dark hair dishevelled. Nick would never be attracted to her; she just wasn't his type. He went for leggy, very glamorous blondes...Natasha would be his type.

She closed her eyes. Why was she thinking like this? She was upset enough without torturing herself with wild imaginings. Maybe it was the brandy she had drunk.

'Are you OK?' Nick's gentle voice made her eyes fly open again.

'Yes...'

He put the T-shirt down on the bed.

'Do you mind if I have a shower and turn in?' She looked up at him, her eyes shadowed.

'Of course not. Make yourself at home.'

A few minutes later as Kate stood under the forceful jet of the shower and poured shampoo on her hair, she dismissed the way she had thought about Nick. Her body was in shock—she wasn't thinking rationally, never mind clearly. It was Stephen whom she had loved. And now it was over.

She stepped out of the shower and towel-dried her body. How long had he been having an affair? Did any of their other friends know? Tanya and David had come around for dinner last week and, come to think of it, Tanya had been quiet, very unlike her usual gregarious self. As Tanya worked with Stephen, presumably she knew Natasha.

Kate's stomach churned. The more she thought about it, the more convinced she was that Tanya knew. Those looks she had been giving her over the dinner table had been looks of sympathy.

She groaned. How many other people knew? She felt like a total idiot.

'Kate, I've brought you a drink.' Nick's voice coming from the bedroom made her jump. She wrapped a towel around herself and opened the door.

Nick was putting a coffee and a sandwich down on the bedside table.

'You shouldn't have done that, Nick.' She tucked the edge of the white towel down firmly. 'It's very kind, but I honestly don't think I can eat anything.'

'You're skin and bone as it is.' His eyes flicked momentarily over her, taking in the long, shapely legs. 'You can't afford to skip meals.'

'Yes, I can.' She sighed. 'But thanks for the compliment.'

'It wasn't a compliment.' He grinned. 'Come on, eat this and make me happy.'

'Hold on a minute.' She snatched up the T-shirt from the bed and retired into the bathroom again. Did Nick really think she was too thin? she wondered as she took off the towel and slipped into the white cotton shirt. Come to think about it, maybe he did prefer his women with a more curvy shape. Serena had been very well endowed.

Irritated that she was even thinking along these lines, Kate turned her attention to her appearance. The T-shirt was big on her and came down nearly to her knees. She gave her hair a quick blast with the hairdryer so that it sat in glossy waves around her face. Then she surveyed her reflection in the mirror; she looked a bit better, she supposed. There was a bit of colour in her cheeks now, and her eyes weren't quite as puffy. Not that she really cared how she looked for Nick…it was just female vanity.

When she returned to the bedroom she found Nick sitting on the bed watching the small TV set which was on a stand at the far side of the room.

'Nothing on, as usual,' he said, flicking through the channels. He gave her a cursory glance before returning his attention back to the set.

She needn't have bothered worrying about how she looked, she thought as she climbed onto the bed and sat behind him, reaching for the coffee.

'Don't forget your sandwiches.' He grinned at her. 'You'll have nightmares if you don't eat something.'

'I'll probably have those anyway,' she muttered glumly. 'I'll probably see Natasha and Stephen walking down the aisle, hand in hand.'

'That sounds like Stephen's nightmare, not yours,' he muttered dryly.

'Just because you are frightened of commitment, doesn't mean every man is,' Kate retorted sharply.

'So you think Stephen is suddenly going to turn into Mr Commitment, do you? Mr Fidelity?'

Kate shrugged and took a sip of her drink. 'I don't know what Stephen is going to do. I don't think I know him any more.'

Nick switched off the TV and turned to look at her. 'Get real, Kate. Stephen is having a fling. It probably won't last two minutes.'

'How do you figure that out?'

'Well, for one thing he can hardly keep a job down for two minutes, never mind a relationship.'

'We lived together for two years, Nick. Stephen isn't that flaky.'

'That's a matter of opinion,' Nick retorted dryly.

'At least he tried to settle down.'

'Unlike me, you mean?'

'I didn't say that.'

'That's what it sounded like.'

She frowned. Were they arguing? She and Nick never argued…well, not real arguing—maybe they differed occasionally on small things, but they never snapped at each other. 'I didn't mean it to sound like that,' she said with a shake of her head. 'But, you know, Stephen may not have been the most reliable of people, but he did try to commit…you haven't had a serious relationship since Jayne.'

'Yes, you made that point earlier,' Nick muttered. 'My relationships may not have lasted long, but at least I have always been honest with my girlfriends. I've never lied or cheated.'

'I know—'

'You need to stop romanticizing about Stephen,' Nick cut across her before she could continue. 'You're burying your head in the sand. OK, he may have said he loved you once upon a time, but anyone can pay lip service to emotions. Actions are what matter in the end, and real life isn't like it is in your picture-perfect, idealized dreams.'

Kate swallowed hard. 'Well, I kind of realized that when I saw Stephen in bed with someone else tonight,' she muttered, her eyes shimmering bright green in the glare of the bedside lamp.

Nick watched the tears threaten to spill over from her eyes and groaned. 'I'm sorry, Katy. I shouldn't have said that.'

She shook her head. 'No, you're right. I am too much of a romantic. I know I am.'

'Well, there's nothing wrong with that, I suppose.' Nick's lips twisted ruefully. 'Just don't make excuses for Stephen, OK? It irritates the hell out of me.'

'You never liked him, did you?' she asked tremulously.

Nick shook his head. 'Not much.'

She bit down on her lip and looked away from him.

'Oh, come on, Kate. You've got to admit, there were times when you had no idea where you stood with him. He was inconsistent. One day he was showering you with roses, the next he stood you up.'

Kate was about to argue and say he had never stood her up, and then she remembered how he hadn't turned up for her office party last year. Stephen had apologized profusely the next day, though…said he had been held up in a rehearsal with the band.

'He had a bit of an artistic temperament, I suppose,' she muttered.

'You mean he loved himself more than anyone else.'

'I don't know,' she murmured. She finished her coffee and then leaned back against the headboard, stretching her long legs out in front of her on the white bedspread. 'What am I going to do, Nick?' she asked him with a sigh. 'I've spent two years of my life working on my relationship with Stephen…what am I going to do now?'

'Get selfish and think about yourself for a while. You're free to do exactly what you want now. Being single can be fun,' he said firmly.

'Can it?' She looked down at her hands. 'To be honest, it feels a bit scary.'

'That's only because events have been forced on you, but you'll be OK.' He reached out and took one of her hands in both of his. 'You're a survivor, Kate, you always have been. You'll cope without Stephen. You managed before he came along, didn't you? You were independent and strong. Hell, you even moved out here from London on your own when you were offered a promotion and you didn't know a soul out here then.'

'That's true. But that seems like a long time ago now, as if it happened to a different person.'

'It's only two and a half years ago. You're still the same person. This is just a set-back, that's all. You'll bounce back.'

'I hope you're right,' she said hesitantly. 'At the moment I feel that things are never going to be the same again.'

'And maybe that's a good thing,' Nick said firmly.

'Maybe it is,' she said, watching the way his hand was resting against hers. She had read somewhere that you could tell a person's personality from their hands. Nick's were large and capable. She felt as if she could bring any problem and put it into Nick's hands and he would fix it for her. She'd always felt like that about Nick—he was strong, nothing fazed him. In contrast, Stephen had always made her feel protective towards him. As if he was the one who'd needed her to look after him. He'd brought his problems to her and she'd fixed them. She had thought he'd needed her, but obviously he hadn't needed her that much…either that or Natasha was fulfilling that role now.

'And when your thoughts do turn to Stephen, remember the bad times. Don't dwell for a second on any of the good. It will make you feel a hell of a lot better.'

'Is that what you did when you and Jayne split up?' she asked curiously, looking up into his eyes.

'Something like that.'

She noticed how he clammed up when she mentioned Jayne. It had always been the same. They could talk about anything and everything, but not Jayne. Kate still didn't know the real reason why that relationship had broken apart and Nick obviously had no intention of telling her.

'She really loved you, you know,' Kate said suddenly, seriously. 'I remember her telling me that a few weeks before your relationship broke up. I remember thinking that she sounded sad, as if she knew it wasn't going to work out between you. It was almost as if she thought you were in love with someone else.'

'And what did you say?' Nick asked quietly.

'I told her to the best of my knowledge there wasn't anyone else. That you cared about her deeply.' Kate hesitated, her eyes thoughtful. 'You weren't cheating on her, were you?'

Nick shook his head.

'What happened?' She looked up at him. 'You went out with her for a long time, Nick, you must have been smitten—so why finish it?'

'Kate, it's in the past, there's no point raking over it. Jayne's probably married with children by now,' he muttered.

She frowned. 'Yes, but that's not the point, is it—?'

'The point is that we all make mistakes—'

'At least you didn't make the mistake of living with Jayne,' she murmured. 'Moving in with Stephen was a big, big mistake, I can see that now.'

'Hey, I've had my share of disastrous relationships.' Nick lightened his tone. 'Remember Rebecca Palmer?'

Kate laughed.

'There you go, I knew I could cheer you up.' Nick's hands left hers. 'Was she off her trolley or what?'

'She was a bit weird.'

'A bit weird, she was seriously scary, and yet when I took her out first time, I thought she was gorgeous.'

'That's because you never look much further than a great body…it doesn't matter about the personality.'

'That's not true.' Nick looked at her with a twinkle in his dark eyes. 'It does matter if they want a second date.'

'You're incorrigible,' Kate muttered. 'You do nothing but break women's hearts. Just as well I never fell in love with you.'

'Why was that, I wonder?' Nick's voice was suddenly contemplative. His eyes moved over her face. 'How come I never added you to my list of conquests?'

Kate shrugged. Suddenly she was very conscious of the fact that she had very little on. The T-shirt was hardly modest—it reached her knees but it was very fine cotton and the shape of her breasts was visible to the discerning eye. And suddenly his eye did seem to be more than a little attentive.

'You're a Gemini and I'm a Sagittarius,' she murmured. 'We wouldn't be compatible.' She moistened her lips as his gaze rested on their softness.

Nick grinned. 'You're not still into that astrology stuff, are you?'

'You may mock, but my stars said this morning that I was entering a phase of profound change.'

'So you think every Sagittarian came home to find their partner had…strayed.'

'Don't be obtuse, Nick. Change takes many forms.'

'Exactly, which is how these astrologers can claim success so often. You can read anything into those columns.'

Kate frowned. 'You're such a sceptic, Nick.'

'And you're such a sucker when it comes to superstition.'

'I rest my case.' She shrugged. 'You're a Gemini and I'm a Sagittarian. We're totally opposite and that's why a relationship would never have worked between us.'

Nick's gaze moved again to her lips. 'I could blow a hole in that theory very easily,' he murmured. There was something dangerously seductive about his words and the way he was looking at her.

She felt her body temperature increase dramatically. 'So...so why don't you?' Kate angled her chin and sent him an unconsciously provocative look from glittering emerald eyes.

'Because now's not the time.' He moved back from her.

About to challenge him to what exactly he meant by that, she changed her mind as he glanced at her again. Maybe some things were better left as they were.

'And anyway, friendship seems to last longer than everything else, doesn't it?' Nick glanced at his watch. 'And given the fact that we are so...opposite in every way...we are lucky to have that in spades, aren't we?'

There was a dry irony in the last part of those words but she decided to ignore it. 'Yes, we are. What time is it?' she asked.

'Almost one, we'd better try and get some sleep.'

'Yes. I suppose we should.'

'Will you be OK now?'

'I'll be fine.' She smiled at him. 'You're right, I am strong and I will bounce back.'

'Not if you don't eat, though.' He pointed to the food beside them on the table. 'Try and have something.'

She nodded.

'See you in the morning, then.' He leaned towards her. Her heart missed a beat as he kissed her on the cheek. She could smell his cologne, feel his warmth. His hand rested lightly on her shoulder, yet she imagined she could feel it burn slightly through the shirt.

'Sleep well,' he said as he got to his feet.

She watched as he left the room and closed the door behind him.

Somehow she just knew that she wouldn't get any sleep at all.

CHAPTER THREE

THE phone was ringing as Kate let herself into her apartment. She wondered if it was Stephen. It was almost six weeks now since he had left and she hadn't heard a thing from him. Most of his clothes were still hanging in the wardrobes; his CDs were still beside the hi-fi. She supposed he would get in contact if only to collect them, but she wished he'd get it over with—this waiting around seemed interminable. It felt as if she were living in no man's land; their relationship was over and yet he was still here in essence. Every time the doorbell or the phone rang her nerves seemed to go into freefall.

She put her shopping down on the kitchen counter and snatched up the receiver.

'Hi, Kate, it's Tanya.'

'Oh, hi, Tanya.' She sat down at the breakfast bar, not knowing if she felt relieved or disappointed that it wasn't him. 'How are you?'

'More to the point, how are you?' Tanya said, sympathy filling her voice and for some reason jarring on Kate. 'I'm really sorry to hear about you and Stephen splitting up.'

'Well, don't be too sorry, it's probably for the best.' Kate tried to sound upbeat. She liked Tanya and they had been friends for a while, but she was very aware that the other woman worked with Stephen and so anything Kate said might be repeated to him.

'So you're really OK?' Tanya sounded surprised.

Did she think I'd fall to pieces? Kate wondered, feeling

35

a tinge of anger. And, if so, why hadn't she rung before now?

'Yes, I'm really fine. In fact I couldn't be better,' Kate purred, her voice exuding a glowing happiness that was completely at odds with her reflection in the mirror opposite. She looked tired, testament to the fact that she hadn't been sleeping very well recently.

'I'm so pleased, Kate. I've wanted to ring you for a while but I've kept putting it off. I feel a bit torn, being friends to both you and Stephen...and also with working with Natasha.'

'There's no need to feel awkward, Tanya,' Kate assured her. 'It's all water under the bridge now and I'm happily getting on with my life.'

'Are you seeing someone else?'

Kate hesitated, wondering how much of this conversation would go back to Stephen. 'Well...you know, I've got a few irons in the fire.' How many more clichés could she use to extract herself from this situation? she asked herself sardonically.

'That's great! Listen, what are you doing the weekend after next?'

'I don't know.' Put on the spot, Kate blustered feebly. 'Nothing much, just the usual—'

'That's brilliant, because David and I are getting married.' Tanya's voice resounded with happiness. 'And I want you to come.'

Kate could feel her temperature rising. She wanted to ask if Stephen and Natasha would be there, but that would go against the relaxed 'I'm over him' attitude, wouldn't it? So instead she resorted to cheerful congratulations, while trying to work out a sensible reply to the invitation. Why hadn't she said she was busy that weekend? Why the hell hadn't she said she was out of town, going to Paris…anything?

'I'm so pleased for you, Tanya,' she heard herself gush.

'Thanks, Kate. I was worried about telling you…what with you and Stephen splitting up. You two had lived together as long as we have…and, well, I felt a bit…awkward.'

'There's no need,' Kate said sincerely. 'I really am happy for you.'

'Yes, I should have known you would be. I'm glad you will be able to come, Kate, it means a lot to me. I'll stick an invitation in the post for you…oh, and bring a partner if you like.'

'Thank you.' Kate didn't know what else to say.

'OK, see you soon. Bye, now.'

Tanya's cheerful tones rang in her ears as she put the phone down. You should have just told her you were busy, that you'd forgotten some important previous engagement, Kate told herself fiercely. You don't want to see Stephen and Natasha. It will be pure torture. On the other hand, why should she stay away? She had been Tanya's friend before Stephen. Hell, on his request she had even pulled the strings to help him get the job there. She had nothing to be ashamed of…unlike Stephen. If he and that woman had any conscience, they would be the ones to stay away.

It crossed her mind that she could ask Nick to accompany her. That would cause a few raised eyebrows. It would also wipe that note of sympathy out of people's voices. No one could feel sorry for her if she had a man as gorgeous as Nick on her arm. She could pretend that he was her lover, they could dance close together on the dance-floor, gaze into each other eyes. That would knock the arrogant smile off Stephen's face. For a moment she felt a burst of happiness at the thought, then the daydream faded into reality. Stephen wouldn't care if she were dating Prince William, and Nick wouldn't want to pretend to be anything but her friend. It would be too embarrassing even to ask him.

Kate glanced at her watch and then got up to put the shopping away. She had better get a move on. She had invited Nick for dinner and he would be arriving in a little over an hour.

The lasagne safely in the oven and the table laid, she went to make herself presentable. She showered and changed into a pale blue skirt and matching top. Then she applied some make-up to hide the dark circles under her eyes and some brighter lipstick.

Not bad, she thought as she ran a smoothing hand over her long dark hair and stepped back to survey her appearance in the full-length mirror. She hadn't seen Nick in a few days. He'd been to Paris on business and she had really missed him.

She didn't think she would have been able to get through these last few weeks if it hadn't been for Nick. Somehow being with him had made things feel better. He'd taken her out quite a bit, to the cinema and for drinks. Of course, she knew he was doing it to cheer her up, but she appreciated it…and it had worked. He had been very good company.

She felt excited at the prospect of spending the evening with him tonight; she glanced at the clock, counting the minutes until he'd arrive, and hoped his flight wasn't delayed.

As Kate made to leave the bedroom she noticed a pile of Stephen's books sitting on the top of a chest of drawers. She really needed to start sorting things out, putting his stuff into boxes and clearing out the debris. She took out an old suitcase from the top of one of the wardrobes and dropped the books inside. Then on impulse she started throwing a few other things in. It felt quite good tossing bits of Stephen into a box—his football kit, his magazines, his dreadful pictures of motor racing. She was starting to enjoy herself when the front doorbell rang.

Nick was standing on the front doorstep, a bouquet of flowers in his hand.

'Hi.' He smiled at her.

'Hi, yourself.' She grinned back at him, feeling happier than she had felt in a long time. 'You're just in time to help me carry a heavy suitcase down the hall.'

'Am I? Whose suitcase is it?'

'Guess?' Kate reached to kiss him on the cheek and was overpowered by the scent of lilies and mimosa. His arms went around her, delaying her momentarily beside him.

'So how are things with you?' He looked deep into her eyes, his gaze moving over her face, noting the hollows beneath her cheeks, the slight shadows under her eyes.

She felt her body tingle with awareness at his closeness. Felt her heart starting to speed up, her pulses race. 'I'm OK, but I'm glad you're back.' Did her voice sound as breathless as she suddenly felt? Perplexed by the rush of adrenalin, she pulled away from him and led the way into the apartment. 'Thanks for the flowers,' she said, burying her face into their sweet scent and breathing deeply.

'It's the least I could do when you've offered to cook me dinner.' Nick grinned. 'So, where's this case you want me to carry out for you?'

'It's in the bedroom. You can do it later.'

As he followed Kate through the smart apartment to the dining room, he noticed that she had lost weight, the pale blue skirt that used to reveal the delightful curves of her hips now hung on her.

'So, what's the news?' he asked. 'Have you heard anything from Stephen?'

'No, I've no news on that front. I just thought I'd make a start and pack up some of his stuff for him so it's ready if he calls by.'

'I'd throw it out if I were you,' Nick muttered.

'I couldn't do that.'

Why not? Nick wondered as he watched her walk through to the kitchen to put the flowers in water. Surely she wasn't still carrying a torch for Stephen after the way he'd treated her? The notion angered him. He wanted to tell her to just forget the guy.

'Anyway, I've started to pack things up, because I'm going to have to move,' she said as she returned to put the vase of flowers on the sideboard. 'This apartment is too expensive for me to manage on my own, so I've had to give in my notice.'

'Oh, Kate, I am sorry. I know how much you love this place.'

The gentleness of his tone made her insides twist with a painful kind of longing. She shrugged. 'Maybe it's for the best. There are a lot of memories here for me, and I'm better to move on, forget them.'

He nodded. 'Have you seen anywhere you like yet?'

'I've only looked through the papers. I'll start in earnest next week.'

'Well, if you're stuck you can always stay in my spare room for a while.'

'Thanks.' She wondered what it would be like to stay at his place. For a moment her mind flicked back to the night she had slept there. She remembered the way she had felt when they had been alone in the bedroom, and how she had forgotten where she was the next morning and raced out into the landing to answer the phone, only to find Nick standing there with a towel around his waist, his hair and his body still glistening damply from the shower.

'It's for me,' he had said calmly as he'd turned and met her eyes.

She had found herself gibbering something, her skin on fire, as she'd wrenched her gaze away from the powerful masculinity of his body.

Kate met his gaze now and felt herself heating up at the memory.

Maybe staying at Nick's place wouldn't be a good idea, she told herself.

She glanced at her watch and tried to bring her thoughts back to reality. 'Help yourself to a drink, Nick. I'll just check on the oven and then you can tell me all about Paris.'

When she came back, Nick had poured them both a glass of red wine.

'How's work?' he asked as he handed her the drink.

'Fine. I'm working with a new author. He writes horror stories with a difference.'

'What's different about them?' He took off his jacket and slung it over the back of a chair.

'The fact that I'm actually enjoying them.' Kate turned and grinned at him, a return to her old good humour lurking in the bright green of her eyes. It had been a source of amusement between them when she had got a job editing horror stories, because she had always disliked the genre.

'Trouble is, they're keeping me up at night.'

'They are so page-turning?'

'No. Every time I hear a noise I have to put the lights

on.' She widened her eyes in mock fear. 'They are scaring the hell out of me. If it carries on like this you are going to have to come and camp on my settee.'

'I've heard some excuses in my time from women wanting me to stay the night, but never one as corny as that,' Nick said with a shake of his head.

'Spoilsport.' Kate laughed.

She sipped the drink and surveyed him over the rim of the glass. He looked tanned and healthy. 'The weather was obviously good in Paris.'

'Not bad.'

'Did you have a walk along the Seine?'

He nodded. 'Only as far as a little restaurant on the Left Bank.'

'That sounds nice.' Kate frowned. Had he been dining on his own? she wondered suddenly. 'It's not like you to make time for enjoying yourself on a business trip.'

'Well, even on a business trip I've got to eat,' Nick said with a grin. 'Speaking of which, there's a very nice smell coming from your kitchen.'

'It's only lasagne.' Kate wished she had been adventurous and cooked something a little more exotic now. 'It should just about be ready. Shall we sit at the table?'

As she carried the food through, Nick turned on the CD player and put on some music. He was very much at home here, Kate thought suddenly as she watched him. Yet she couldn't really say that he was part of the furniture. His presence was too powerful, too disturbingly male.

It was a long time since they had dined alone. Usually when they sat in here it was at a dinner party surrounded by other guests. Was that why she felt a little on edge tonight, suddenly shy in his presence?

'So, did you meet anyone interesting when you were in Paris?' she asked as they started to eat.

'Depends what you mean by interesting,' he answered with a shrug. 'The managing director of the company I'm dealing with at the moment was there.'

'Oh? What was he like?'

'It was a woman, actually. Clare Aidan. She was very nice, very easy to do business with.'

'Was that who you had dinner with?' Kate asked.

'Yes, it was, actually.'

Kate imagined him walking along the Seine with a beautiful woman at his side and felt a prickle of something akin to jealousy stir inside her. The sensation made her most uncomfortable. It was over six weeks since he had split from Serena, she told herself sharply. Of course he was going to start dating other women at some point, she had done well to have him to herself for these last few weeks.

In all honesty, possessiveness wasn't an unusual emotion for Kate where Nick and his girlfriends were concerned. Each time a new woman came into his life she felt the same old twinge inside, and she'd worry for a while if the new relationship would be a threat to their friendship. It was a side of her personality that she didn't really like and always fought down, usually by being extra friendly towards his girlfriends. After all, she wanted Nick to be happy, and she'd no right to feel territorial about their friendship.

'So things are going OK with this company, then?' She forced herself to try and concentrate on the business side of things and not the other woman.

'Yes, they're talking about extending my contract. So things couldn't be going better.' For a while he talked about the work he had done while in Paris, the factories he had visited. Once or twice he mentioned Clare. From what Kate could glean he had a lot of respect for the woman, and had got on well with her. But then Nick got on well with nearly everyone, she supposed.

As the light faded outside, Kate lit the candles on the table and the sideboard. The room flickered in the intimate golden light; it played over Nick's features. He had rugged good looks, she thought absently. His jaw-line was strong, his cheekbones angular, giving a chiselled, almost aristocratic quality to his looks. And his eyes were the most gorgeous shade of hazel-brown. If Clare was any kind of red-blooded female she had probably fallen for him. But as Nick wasn't into commitment she would be wasting her time, Kate reminded herself quickly. The thought was oddly reassuring.

'I have to go out to Stockholm for more talks and there's a possibility they'll want me to go out to the States next month.'

'You'll be having to get yourself a private jet if things carry on like this,' Kate said with a smile. She reached to pour him another cup of coffee.

'Or move to the States.'

Kate nearly dropped the coffee-pot. 'You're not serious?'

Nick shrugged.

She felt like saying, You can't. What will I do without you? But she said nothing. How could she? She had no right to say something like that. 'I'd miss you,' she said simply.

Their eyes met across the table. 'Would you?'

'Of course.' She felt acutely self-conscious as she looked into those dark eyes.

'Well, it's only been mooted so maybe it won't be necessary.' He shrugged. 'Time will tell.'

She supposed she was lucky that he was here with her now. It was only his European contracts that had made him relocate to Amsterdam last year. Most of his work over the last twelve months had been here. But now that he was working with an American firm, was America the logical next step? Things certainly seemed to be taking off for him; he was so much in demand he could barely keep up with the requests on his time.

'I'm pleased that things are going so well for you, Nick.' Kate looked away from him, in case he would see how the thought of him leaving had affected her. 'I was reading your stars this morning and they said things would be looking up for you.'

'Really.' Nick grinned. 'Well, that's a relief.'

She ignored the sarcasm in his tone. 'You may mock, but the guy in the local paper is very accurate. He seems to hit the nail on the head every time for me.'

'Sounds painful.'

She looked over at him. 'Yes, it has been,' she said pointedly.

Nick ignored the reference to the past. 'So what about the future?' he asked instead. 'Has this guy said anything encouraging about romance? Are the stars favourable for that?' He leaned his elbows on the table and rested his chin in his hands, fixing Kate with a direct look across the candlelit table that for some reason made her blush.

'Who for?' She took a sip of coffee. 'You or me?'

'Both of us.'

She shrugged and the uncomfortable thought came into her head that maybe he was wondering how his chances stood with the marvellous Clare. 'He didn't say anything about my love life. But I told you…things are good for you.'

'Really? How good?'

She hesitated. 'Let me see…I can't really remember.' Why was she lying? she asked herself with a frown. She could remember all too clearly. Heaven's sake, he's not going to dash off into Clare's arms because of a few lines of a horoscope, she told herself sternly. He didn't even believe in them. 'Apparently you're going to start a new relationship…' she told him hesitantly. 'You're going to meet someone at a party.'

'A party?' Nick grinned. 'Well, as I haven't had any invitations to a party, I won't hold my breath.'

'You could come to one with me.' The words popped out before she could think about them. 'I've been invited to Tanya and David's wedding.'

Nick frowned. 'Doesn't Tanya work with Stephen?'

Kate nodded.

'Is that why you want to go to the wedding—because Stephen will be there?'

'No! Of course not, and, anyway, even if he is there he'll be with Natasha.'

'So you want me there for moral support?'

'No…well, yes, I suppose so.' She frowned, wondering where the relaxed atmosphere between them had gone. Nick seemed to be looking at her as if she had sprouted a forked tongue.

'You need to let go of the past, Kate,' he said seriously.

'I have let go of the past. But it's only six weeks since Stephen and I split up—I'm bound to be a bit apprehensive about seeing him again.'

Nick said nothing to that, just continued to look at her with those dark, somehow disturbing eyes.

'I'm not sure if I really want to go to the wedding anyway, but Tanya was insistent and I wasn't quick enough to think of an excuse,' she continued quickly.

'When is it?'

'The weekend after next. I don't know where the venue is. She said she'd put an invitation in the post.' She held his gaze steadily. 'My first instinct was that I definitely didn't want to go, but then I thought, Tanya was my friend before I even met Stephen and why should I stay away? I've got nothing to be ashamed of.'

'No, you haven't.'

'But you don't think I should go?'

'What I think isn't important.' There was that tone in his voice again, it sounded like disapproval. 'If you want to go, and you don't think it will upset you, then go.'

'I don't know how it will affect me to see Stephen again,' Kate murmured honestly, and for a moment her eyes were shadowed, distant. 'I won't go if you can't come with me,' she said.

'And in what capacity do you want me there?'

'Capacity?' She stared at him blankly.

'Am I there as your friend or your lover?'

The husky question made confusion and heat rise inside Kate as she remembered her earlier thoughts. 'Well…as my friend—'

'So if this gorgeous woman that I'm predicted to meet at a party is there, you won't mind if I move in on her?'

Kate felt her cheeks colour. 'No, of course not.' But even as she spoke she knew she was lying. She would mind very much.

'OK, then, count me in. That's if I'm free, of course. I'll have to check my schedule.'

Why was he being so obtuse? she wondered irritably. Why couldn't he just smile and say, Yes, if I'm free, of course I'll come with you, instead of making such a big deal out of it? 'You sound like a veritable entrepreneur.' Kate couldn't keep the acerbic bite out of her voice.

'And you sound annoyed,' Nick said calmly.

'Annoyed?' She shook her head. 'Why would I be annoyed?'

He fixed her with an amused look. 'I don't know. You either don't like the sound of my becoming an entrepreneur, or you don't like the sound of me making a move on some gorgeous woman at the party.'

'What rubbish.' She got up and started to clear the table. She was annoyed that he could read her so clearly. But then she supposed that was the downside of knowing someone for so long—they got to know the tell-tale signs, and before you knew where you were they were analysing every flicker of your eyes with frightening accuracy.

Nick got up to help her carry dishes into the kitchen. 'And as you've always been pleased about my business successes I can only conclude it's the latter that has caused you concern.'

'Honestly, Nick, I don't know what you are talking about.'

'So you weren't hoping I was going to play the part of your lover to the gallery of friends and ex-friends at this wedding?'

'No. I wouldn't expect you to do something like that.' Kate straightened from stacking the dishwasher and caught his eye. She felt herself blush. 'All right, it did cross my mind momentarily,' she murmured reluctantly. 'But it was a crazy idea. My pride took a bit of a battering when Stephen left and, yes, for a crazy second I was thinking that I'd enjoy rubbing his nose in the fact that I was happy without him...that someone else wanted me even if he doesn't.'

Nick's dark eyes held hers. 'Playing a game like that could have serious consequences.'

'Could it?' She felt her heart miss a beat. 'What kind of serious consequences?'

Nick shrugged. 'I'd say it would be a bit like throwing a pebble in a pond and watching the ripple effect.'

Kate frowned. 'I don't follow you—'

'Well, have you thought it through?' Nick asked calmly. 'You're hoping to make Stephen jealous—'

'No, I'm not—'

'Oh, come on, Katy. Be honest. There is a bit of that in the equation, isn't there? And just say you succeed? Just say Stephen is eaten up with jealousy?'

Kate shrugged.

'Are you hoping he'll want to come back?'

'I wouldn't have him back!'

Nick looked sceptical.

'I wouldn't,' she said vehemently. 'How could I trust him again?'

'If he worked his charm and said he was sorry—'

'It would take more than that,' Kate assured him firmly.

Nick's eyes glittered in the reflection of the light from the other room. 'I still think it's a dangerous game.'

'But you'd play it...if I asked you?'

He didn't answer her for a moment.

'Nick?' She frowned.

'Yes...I said I'd do it. If I'm here.'

Kate smiled. 'Thanks.'

'But don't say I haven't warned you.' Nick reached out a hand and tipped her chin up so that he could look into her eyes. 'Toying with emotions is always dangerous.'

'You're not worried that Stephen will thump you, are you?' Kate tried to make light of the situation, but there were warning signals. Not least the rapid pulse that beat under the gentle pressure of his fingers.

'I can honestly say that's one scenario that hadn't oc- curred to me.' His lips twitched with amusement.

'Because Stephen wouldn't believe there was anything between us,' Kate murmured flatly, pulling away from the touch of his hand, feeling for some reason upset by the amusement in his tone. 'I suppose you're right. He knows very well that you're my best friend. That there's no spark of attraction between us.'

'Does he?' Nick's voice was dry.

'And he wouldn't care if there was. You haven't seen Natasha. She's stunning.'

'Really. Well, I'll reserve judgement until I've seen her.'

She watched as he walked through to pick up his jacket from the dining room. 'Are you going?'

'Yes, I'd better as it's getting late. Do you want me to help you with that suitcase before I leave?'

'If you wouldn't mind…thanks.'

Kate walked with him down towards the bedroom and wondered if it was her imagination or was the atmosphere between them tense?

'Will I see you after work tomorrow at the café?' she asked.

'I'm going to be pretty tied up tomorrow. It might be better if I give you a ring when I get this next business trip over with.'

The bedroom was in semi-darkness but she didn't bother to switch on the overhead light. She bent down to zip up the case so that he could lift it and Nick sat on the edge of her bed and watched her.

She looked very pale in the soft lamplight and kind of fragile. He wondered how much sleep she had lost over that bastard Stephen. He wished to hell she could forget him. 'You should just let me put this in the back of my car and throw it in the trash,' he said, reaching to help her push the lid down.

Kate shook her head. 'It's not mine to throw away,' she said softly.

'If it meant anything to him, don't you think he would have been back for it by now?'

She shrugged but made no reply.

He watched her for a moment longer as she struggled to fasten her side of the case. He shouldn't say anything about Stephen, he told himself tersely. It was early days and she was bound to still be feeling raw. She needed time and space to get over him. Yet for all his calm reasoning, he felt annoyance bubbling inside him. That crack in the kitchen about Stephen never believing there could be a spark between them had just about finished him off. He was sick of hearing about the guy.

The careful way she was trying to pull the zip over his belongings was irritating him too.

'Here, get out of the way and I'll do it.' He got down beside her on the floor and pulled the suitcase around, closing it with a roughness that made something inside crack.

'Be careful Nick!'

He glanced over at her, his dark eyes angry. 'You are too damn soft sometimes, do you know that?'

'No, I'm not.'

He tossed her a scathing look. 'You need to forget Stephen Harrington ever existed and get rid of everything that belonged to him.'

'I don't need you to tell me what to do, Nick.' Kate glared at him. 'And I am forgetting about Stephen.'

'If you were forgetting about Stephen you'd have thrown his stuff in the bin and you wouldn't be wasting your time trying to think of ways to make him jealous.'

'If you're referring to my going to Tanya's wedding with you, you can forget about it. It was a passing thought and not a very good one at that. No one would believe we were lovers anyway.'

'Wouldn't they?' For a moment Nick's voice was low, almost dangerously quiet. 'Are you trying to issue some kind of a challenge?' He finished fastening the case and stood up.

'No, of course not…look, let's not argue.' She stood up as well, brushing down her skirt, feeling nervous suddenly. She couldn't work out what had changed between them. Over dinner it had been pleasant and light-hearted, the next minute they were into uncharted territory and she didn't know how to deal with it.

'Good. Because I think I could put up quite a persuasive act,' Nick said quietly.

'What kind of persuasive act?' Kate asked guardedly.

His eyes moved towards her lips. Suddenly she felt hot all over. Her breathing was constricted; her heart was hammering unmercifully against her chest.

She could have moved away from him as he stepped closer. But she couldn't seem to operate her limbs; she just stood there, looking up at him, waiting breathlessly.

'What kind of act do you think?' Nick put his hand around her waist and pulled her against him. Then he lowered his head towards her.

Her heart skipped crazily about in her chest, butterflies of apprehension and excitement fluttering wildly out of control. He gave her ample opportunity to pull away from him, but she didn't. She put her hand against his shoulder but it wasn't to push him away.

Kate had never been this close to him before. Their lips were inches apart, and she could feel his breath warm against her skin. It made the fine hair at the back of her neck prickle, and a searing awareness of his sensuality soar through her. She wanted him to kiss her; she moistened her lips, feeling herself tremble inside with anticipation.

He bent his head and his lips touched hers. It was a gentle kiss to begin with, just a seductive caress that made her hungry for more. She tentatively slid her hand further up his shoulder, and stood on tiptoe. She was half scared by what they were doing...yet she thrilled at the way his lips dominated hers, and as the kiss deepened a hunger stirred inside that completely overrode any prudent concerns. Suddenly she was responding to him with a recklessness that was totally unrestrained.

She felt his hand move under her top and stroke across the naked skin of her back. Her breasts felt heavy and sensitised as they pressed against his chest. She longed for his hands to move, for him to caress her totally.

The bed was behind them and it would be so easy to just fall back against it and give in to the urgent demands her body was suddenly making. She wanted him so much, it was like an overwhelming tidal wave of desire and all she could do was move with it.

When he moved back from her she was left breathless, shaken and very disappointed. She'd wanted him to continue. She looked up at him with eyes that were wide with shock and confusion.

His lips twisted in a half-smile. 'Do you think something like that would be convincing?'

The humour that laced his deep tone hit some sensitive nerve. She felt hurt, which was crazy. That kiss had unleashed some kind of emotional storm inside her. All right, it was completely wrong to feel like this. Nick was her friend...her best friend. But she couldn't help it. The fact that he could kiss her with such passion and feel nothing was a shock.

She shrugged, and for a moment she couldn't find her voice. She felt breathless, dizzy with a desire that was slow to fade. 'Maybe…maybe you shouldn't have done that,' she murmured at last.

His smile was cool. 'You issued a challenge, Katy—'

'No, I didn't.' She felt the colour deepen in her cheeks.

The look he levelled at her was deeply sardonic. 'If you play with fire, you should expect to get burnt.'

'I don't know what you're talking about, Nick.' Her voice trembled alarmingly.

'Yes, you do.' He turned away from her and picked up the suitcase from the floor. 'Where do you want me to put this?'

The change of subject and tone made her blink. 'In the hall cupboard.'

Kate followed him down the hall. She wanted to say something witty or pragmatic, something to let him know that the kiss was forgotten, that it was a joke and she recognized it as such. But she didn't know what to say.

Nick tossed the suitcase in the cupboard and turned to look at her. 'Are you OK now?' he asked coolly.

'Of course I'm OK.'

'Good.' He smiled.

Despite the casualness of his attitude, there was awkwardness between them, which Kate felt extremely aware of. Maybe it was her? Maybe it was all in her head?

'I'll speak to you soon. Thanks for dinner.'

Kate watched as he walked towards his car, unlocking it with a press of a button. She waited as he started the ignition with a roar and drove away, and even managed to give a cheerful wave as he went past her. But as soon as he had disappeared her smile slipped.

She turned back to her apartment. Despite the warm summer evening she felt cold, then she remembered the way Nick had kissed her and felt hot. She headed for the bathroom and ran some cold water to splash her face. As

Kate waited for the basin to fill she studied her reflection in the mirror. Her lips were still slightly swollen from the heat of Nick's caress. She ran a finger gently over them, a feeling of bewilderment and wonder churning inside her.

CHAPTER FOUR

KATE tossed and turned in the large double bed.

'Are you trying to issue some kind of a challenge?' Nick's words echoed through her head.

'No, of course not.' Her own reply wavered unconvincingly.

Then she felt the heat of his lips against hers, warm, sensitive, turning her insides to lava. No one had ever kissed her like that before.

'Nick.' She whispered his name into the darkness, her body aching with desire, wanting more... She felt his hands against her naked skin, felt her body tightening, tingling...yearning.

The shrill ring of the alarm clock made her eyes fly open; her heart was thudding, her body hot. She felt disorientated.

'It was a dream,' she murmured, trying in some way to reassure herself. Except that it wasn't a dream. Nick really had kissed her like that. But that had been over a week ago, and she hadn't seen him since. Surely she could just forget about it now? Kate closed her eyes again, trying to rid herself of the feeling of arousal, and emptiness.

She had to be honest: there had been times in the past when she had wondered what it would be like to kiss Nick. She had always suspected that it would be pleasurable, but she hadn't imagined just *how pleasurable*.

She couldn't jeopardize her friendship with Nick by giving credence to these feelings, she told herself sternly.

Their friendship was too precious and too special to wreck it by an act of indiscretion, and that was all this could be.

Nick was a red-blooded male, she had thrown down a challenge—albeit mistakenly—and he had responded. But he wasn't really attracted to her. He had made that pretty clear after he had kissed her. It had had no effect on him whatsoever.

Which was more than could be said of her!

'What's the matter with me?' she groaned. She threw the covers of the bed back and went to have a shower.

It was a good thing that Nick had been away on business this last week. It would be too humiliating by far if he guessed how one little kiss had disturbed her equilibrium.

Things could never work between her and Nick. Kate stood under the forceful jet of water and washed her hair as she counted the reasons why they could never work out. They were total opposites, for heaven's sake, and he was... She was going to tell herself he was like a brother to her, but the words stuck and refused to ring clearly or convincingly inside her. Instead she found herself remembering the heat of his kiss again. She tried to push the memory very firmly to the back of her mind.

She respected Nick and liked him too much to think like this...plus she needed him as her friend. And if anything happened between them, it would ruin everything.

She had to put things right, but how? Even the sound of his voice when he'd rung her yesterday to tell her he was home had sent her blood pressure rising. They'd arranged to meet for coffee after work. He'd sounded totally matter of fact. Obviously he wasn't dwelling on the stupid kiss, so neither should she, she told herself crossly.

'I'll tell him today that I've changed my mind about going to the wedding,' Kate said loudly as she dried her-

self. Yes, that would be a good first step towards backing
away from danger. The invitation from Tanya had arrived
last week. The venue was Stevengar, a small village on
the coast about forty miles away. It was her perfect excuse
for not attending, being so far away she would have to
book herself into a hotel and arrange transport. She'd ring
Tanya and tell her she couldn't make it.

And the next step she should take was to start dating
again.

Maybe that was what was wrong with her. She was
missing Stephen, and feeling lonely and vulnerable…
yes…yes, that was it. She clung to the excuse as she had
wanted to cling to Nick when he'd kissed her.

She felt a lot better by the time she set out for work.
It was a fresh, perfect morning, holding the promise of a
scorching day ahead. The sky was a pale blue as if it had
just been newly washed. The scent of the sea was in the
air. Kate took a deep breath as she cycled along the roads.
They were quiet, just a few bicycles hurrying along the
leafy lanes. She cut across one of the canals that criss-
crossed the city. It had a dreamy quality at this time of
the morning. There was a mist hanging over the water, a
mist that would disperse as the sun gained strength.

The rumble of a tram disturbed the peaceful morning.
It sent a flurry of birds flapping up into the sky. Kate
hummed to herself. Suddenly she felt happy for the first
time since Stephen had gone. Why was that? she wondered.

She glanced at her watch. She was early. She could call
on Nick on the way past and tell him about the wedding
being held in Stevengar. He might make her a coffee. She
would look at him and all those stupid thoughts about that
kiss would disappear and once more he would just be

good old Nick, her friend…nothing else. Then again, maybe he would think she had designs on him if she called this early…and after the way she had responded to that kiss, she had better play things carefully. Firmly she steered herself away from Nick's place. A little discretion was called for.

The office was in the usual state of Monday morning turmoil—phones ringing, stacks of post arriving and a problem with the air-conditioning led to a stifling and rather hectic start to the working day—but Kate ignored it all, concentrating on the manuscript in front of her with determination.

'It's hard to breathe in here, let alone work,' her colleague Jan complained as she tried to open the window behind them.

'Electrician should be here in a minute.' Kate jotted down a few notes, and asked abstractedly, 'How was your weekend?'

'Don't ask…I went to the party from hell. Everyone was standing around in tight little cliques, bitching about people behind their backs. Plus there wasn't one eligible man there.'

'Sounds awful,' Kate sympathized.

'How was your weekend?'

'It was OK, quiet but pleasant.'

'Not heard anything from Stephen?'

Kate shook her head. She didn't like to talk about her private life at work and had only mentioned that she and Stephen had split up because there was a work's function next week and the director of the company had wanted to know exactly how many people would be attending.

'So, no man in your life, then?' Jan asked.

'No. Unless you count Nick,' Kate answered absently. 'But that's just platonic.'

'Nick?'

'My friend who has the computer business.'

'Oh, yes.' Jan frowned. 'What's he like?'

'He's a really nice guy.'

'Good-looking?'

'Very.'

'Well, go on…?' Jan prompted curiously.

'He's thirty-three, single, successful and incredibly handsome. There's nothing much else to say.'

'But there's nothing romantic between you?'

'Heavens, no, he's my best friend.' Was her voice a little too emphatic, a little over-zealous?

'Maybe you could introduce me to him?'

The firm note of interest in Jan's voice made Kate look over at her.

Jan was an extremely attractive woman. In fact, it suddenly struck her that she was probably everything that Nick would like: blonde, twenty-six, fabulous figure with long legs.

'Of course,' Kate murmured, not completely enamoured with the idea. Blind dates rarely worked out, she told herself. And even though Jan was lovely, Nick probably wouldn't thank her for trying to fix him up with one of her friends.

'But he's out of town a lot on business. It's hard to catch him.'

'Are you sure you're not interested in the guy yourself?' Jan asked suddenly.

'No! Don't be silly,' Kate cut across her hastily. 'There's nothing between Nick and I…except friendship, of course.' She was babbling; she could hear her voice rising slightly, could feel a tinge of panic entering her tone as from nowhere the memory of his kiss hit her. 'Listen, I'm meeting him for coffee after work,' she found herself saying, desperate to prove to herself and to Jan that what she was saying was the truth. 'Why don't you tag along?'

'I'd like that, thanks.'

Kate smiled and returned her attention to her work. She'd done the right thing, she told herself sternly. Bringing Jan along with her today would be a stroke of genius: it would prove to herself and Jan that there was nothing between her and Nick. And also it would prove to Nick that, despite the heat of her response to him last week, she wasn't harbouring any foolish notions. Things would be back to normal and that old easy comradeship would once again be there between them.

'Here he is now.' From their vantage point at the edge of the pavement café, Kate saw Nick drive up and park. She felt tension mount as she watched him climbing out of his sports car.

He's just Nick, good old Nick, she told herself. The kiss is forgotten—we'll probably even laugh about it in years to come.

She heard Jan's sharp intake of breath and glanced over at her.

'Hell, Kate! He's absolutely gorgeous!' Jan's eyes were riveted on Nick as he strolled across the road.

'Yes, I told you he was.'

'I think I'm in love.'

Kate frowned. 'You don't even know him.'

'I don't need to know him.' Jan wrenched her eyes away from Nick. 'Do I look OK?' she asked urgently, running a hand through her short blonde hair. 'Is my hair all right?'

'Yes, your hair is fine.' Kate bit back a sudden urge to tell the woman to pull herself together.

'Kate, do me a favour, and don't linger over your coffee.'

Kate frowned.

'Oh, go on, please! It will give me a chance to be alone with him.'

'Listen, Jan, I think I should warn you that Nick is a bit of a free spirit. He's not into commitment and he's got an eye for the women—'

'Kate, I'm a big girl.' Jan laughed. 'I can look after myself.'

Kate didn't have time to answer that because as she glanced up she met Nick's eyes across the tables.

Despite the warmth of the late afternoon sun on her back, she felt a delicious kind of a shiver rush down her spine.

Jan was right—he was gorgeous. He was wearing a light-coloured suit teamed with a contrasting light shirt that was open at the neck. The look was very modern and, combined with the dark hair and tanned skin, seemed stylishly Latin. But it's just Nick, she told herself fiercely. Just Nick. The trouble was, as she met his eyes all she could remember was the way he'd kissed her, the way his hand had stroked over her naked skin.

His eyes flicked over Jan, and then rested back on her, his smile cool. 'Hi, sorry I'm a bit late, I had to go out of town today.'

'That's OK, we've only just got here anyway.' Kate tried to sound as laid back as he did. 'This is my friend, Jan. We work together. Jan, this is Nick Fielding.'

'Hi.' The smile Nick bestowed on Jan was warm and charming. Kate could almost see Jan lapping it up, like a flower in a warm summer shower after a very long drought. He pulled out a chair and sat down beside the other woman.

'And how have things been in the world of Temple and Tanner Publishing today?' he asked jovially.

'Not bad, except for the lack of air-conditioning. Oh, and our computer system went down,' Jan replied. 'We could have done with ringing you. You're into computers, aren't you?'

'I am and, if I'd been in town, I'd have rode in to the rescue with pleasure.'

'And we'd have been most grateful,' Jan purred huskily as she crossed her legs. She was wearing a blue dress and it had ridden up a little, revealing tanned very shapely legs; something that hadn't escaped Nick's notice, Kate noted.

'In fact, I'm surprised you haven't been down to our office. You should pop in some time and we'll show you around, make you a coffee.' She glanced over at Kate. 'We'd make him very welcome, wouldn't we, Kate?'

'As long as you're not in a hurry for the coffee,' Kate murmured, thinking about the chaos in their office today. Had Jan taken leave of her senses?

'Are you working in the same section as Kate?' Nick asked nonchalantly. 'The horror crypt?'

Jan's laugh was perhaps a little too hearty. 'No, I edit cookery books and self-help books.'

She could do with one of those self-help books now, Kate thought wryly. *How not to throw yourself at men.* As soon as the thought crossed her mind she was annoyed with herself. Jan was a nice person and, in fairness to her, Nick was extremely charismatic.

'Do you try out the recipes at home?' Nick was asking now.

'Not all of them, but a few; I'm a very good cook.'

Kate watched how coyly Jan fluttered her eyelashes at Nick. Her whole body was angled towards him. If Nick could read body language, Jan's was shouting availability. Did Nick find her attractive? Kate wondered. He seemed to.

The waitress interrupted them to take their order.

'So, where did you go today?' Kate asked Nick once the waitress left.

'Out to the Tate factory, to look at their computer systems.'

Before Kate could continue Jan leaned forward. 'Are you talking about Max Tate?' she asked with interest.

'Yes, that's right.'

'I know Max very well; his daughter is an old friend of mine.'

Kate suppressed a smile. Jan knew everyone; she seemed to spend her life networking, collecting names and people as some would collect stamps. 'In fact it's her birthday on Saturday, and her father is throwing a massive party for her.'

'That's right,' Nick said easily. 'He gave me an invite, as a matter of fact.'

'I've been invited too. Now isn't that a coincidence? We must be destined to meet again, Nick.' She slanted him that look from beneath her eyelashes again. That 'I'm available, come and get me' look.

Kate watched her with a kind of reluctant fascination. Jan reminded her of that old saying, '"come into my parlour," said the spider to the fly.' There was certainly nothing subtle about her approach. Nick would be running in the opposite direction if she didn't cool it.

Their coffee arrived. The pavement café was crowded; there was a relaxed atmosphere, everyone enjoying the sunshine, the food and drink. But for some reason Kate couldn't relax at all.

As Nick and Jan laughed and talked easily together,

she was starting to feel more and more on edge. Probably lack of sleep these last few nights, she thought. But Jan's flirtatious manner and her over-enthusiastic giggle were starting to really grate on her.

She glanced across at Nick, and, finding his attention was trained wholly on Jan, she allowed herself to study him unreservedly. He had always been very good-looking. She remembered at college how the girls had used to swoon when he'd arrived; she'd found it amusing, but she'd always been tremendously proud that she'd been the one he'd sought out.

Kate remembered further back to school and how a boy had grabbed hold of her in the playground and tried to kiss her. Nick had grabbed him by the scruff of his collar and threatened to knock his lights out. She smiled at the memory.

Nick glanced over at her and their eyes met. She felt oddly out of breath, as if she were on a fairground ride and her body were about to be tipped head over heels.

'It is this weekend, isn't it?' he asked.

'Sorry?' She blinked and the spell—or whatever it was that had held her—was broken and she realized she hadn't been listening to a word that had been said.

'Jan's just suggested that we go to the party at Max's together. But I'm taking you to a wedding this weekend coming, aren't I?'

Kate hesitated. This was her cue to say, It's OK, you go to the party with Jan. I don't want to go to that wedding anyway. Only that wasn't what came out. 'Yes, it's this weekend,' she found herself saying calmly. 'And I think we might have to book a hotel, because it's out at Stevengar. If that's all right with you?'

'Yes, fine.' Nick shrugged and looked back at Jan. 'Never mind, another time,' he said easily.

Was it her imagination or was Jan looking at her reproachfully?

Guilt stole over her. What had happened to her sensible intentions this morning about not attending that wedding? She needed to keep away from Stephen—and Nick—until her emotions were back to something approaching normality.

She finished her coffee and glanced over at Nick again. He smiled at her.

'My brother phoned this morning,' he said.

'Oh? How is Josh?'

'Same as ever, overloaded with work. We were discussing Mum and Dad's ruby wedding anniversary next month. He was thinking about throwing a surprise party for them; Rachael has said she can come over from Australia and I'll fly over, of course. We were wondering if you'd like to come…seeing as you are part of the family, so to speak.'

'I'd love to.' Kate's happy smile slipped a little as she glanced over at Jan. She was pointing to her watch and making covert little gestures behind Nick's back, making it obvious that she was waiting for her to leave.

It crossed her mind briefly to just ignore her—she didn't want to leave—but maybe that was selfish. She'd already gone against her better instincts by asking Nick to take her to this wedding.

'Thanks for the invite, Nick, maybe you can tell me about it later?' she said hastily as she glanced back at him. 'I've got to go, unfortunately. I'm…I'm expecting a phone call at home.' It was the only excuse that sprung to mind and she hoped it didn't sound too lame.

Jan smiled at her gratefully as she stood up.

'See you tomorrow.' Kate looked at Nick as he also

stood up, and for a crazy moment she thought he intended to leave with her.

'I'll speak to you later,' he said.

Of course he wasn't going to come with her, she told herself crossly. He was going to sit and bask in the sunshine and Jan's flirtatious company, and she couldn't blame him.

Nick leaned across to kiss her goodbye. The scent of his cologne, his closeness, brought vivid memories of their kiss rushing back to taunt her, and she found herself turning her head awkwardly so that his lips airbrushed against her hair.

'Bye, now.' She smiled uncertainly up at him. Why couldn't she just forget the way he'd kissed her? She wanted everything to be all right between them again, but for some strange reason it felt as if it never would be. The notion made her very unhappy.

'Shall we order another drink?' Kate heard Jan ask as she walked away.

'I don't see why not,' Nick replied nonchalantly as he returned to his seat.

He watched Kate as she hurried across the busy road. She was wearing a fuchsia-pink dress that was summery and feminine; it swirled around her legs as she moved. There was something very set about the rigidity of her back, and the way she didn't glance around or wave as she reached the bridge where her bicycle was chained up. Kate usually waved at that point, or tossed him a parting smile across the crowds.

'Is Kate OK?' he asked Jan.

'She's fine,' Jan answered swiftly, and then hesitated. 'Apart from being devastated over Stephen, of course. I think that's why she's rushing home—she's got an idea in her head that he might ring tonight.'

'I see.' Nick frowned. 'That's bad news.'

'Why? Wouldn't you like to see them getting back together?' Jan asked curiously.

'No.' Nick's answer was blunt. 'I don't like the guy, never have.'

'Oh!' Jan was silent for a moment, before continuing briskly, 'Well, she's still in love with him, and she's been very unhappy since he left, so I think it would be for the best if he did come back.'

Kate decided on an early night. She had a bath, washed her hair and slipped between scented sheets. After all the nights of disturbed sleep she should have flaked out the moment her head hit the pillow, but, perversely, sleep evaded her. She glanced at the bedside clock. It was almost ten. She wondered if Nick was still out with Jan. Maybe they'd gone to a nightclub? Maybe back to her place.

She reached and switched out the light. It was none of her business where they were, she told herself angrily. But it didn't stop her thinking about it. She felt lonely suddenly.

A few moments later the shrill sound of the telephone made her reach blindly out, knocking books and the lamp over in her haste to pick up the receiver.

'Hello?'

'Hello, dear, it's only me.' Her mother's clear tones rang loudly in her ear. 'Just ringing to see how you are. I don't suppose you've heard anything from Stephen?'

Kate stifled a groan, she was in no mood for the third degree and she knew that was what her mother wanted. Let's analyse the situation again, let's go over it in detail and find out exactly what went wrong and where.

'Things are just the same,' Kate murmured.

'I always knew that man was trouble.'

'Did you?' Kate almost wished now she hadn't rung last week to tell her mother about the break-up. Helen Murray had taken the news very badly. Kate hadn't heard her this angry since the days when Kate's father had left. In fact her mother was almost angrier than she was, and it just made Kate feel worse that, not only had her relationship failed, but she'd upset her mother into the bargain.

Even over a long-distance phone call from London she could hear the steam coming out of her mother's ears. 'I knew he was trouble when you told me he played in a rock band. And, in all honesty Kate, it should have told you something.'

What should it have told me? Kate wondered. 'He only played in a rock band as a hobby, Mum,' she said wearily. 'He wasn't Mick Jagger.'

'There you go, standing up for him again—'

'I'm not standing up for him.'

'I should hope not. You need to forget about him Kate.'

'You sound like Nick.'

'How is Nick?' Distracted from her theme, her mother brightened considerably.

'He's fine. I had coffee with him earlier.'

'Such a nice guy. Is he still with Serena?'

'No, the relationship finished a while ago.'

'Really? Now, you could do with finding someone like him to settle down with. You should never have moved in with Stephen—'

Kate cut across her briskly before they could get back to that subject. 'Listen, Mum, I'm going to have to go. There's someone at the door.' She crossed her fingers and hoped a bolt of lightning wouldn't strike her down for telling white lies, but she really was in no mood for this.

'I hope it's not that rat—'

'No, it won't be Stephen. I'll phone you tomorrow.'

It was a relief to put the receiver down. On impulse she unplugged the phone from the wall. Then she leaned her head back against the pillows with a sigh.

Her mother was right; she should never have fallen for Stephen. She closed her eyes and tried to relax.

Despite all her efforts sleep refused to come. Nearly an hour later she was staring at the ceiling counting the swirls in the wallpaper when the doorbell rang.

The sound made Kate jump. That will teach you to lie to your mother, she murmured to herself as she reached for her dressing gown. She hoped to heaven it wasn't Stephen.

Putting on her dressing gown, she hurried down the hall and peered through the side window.

Nick was standing on the doorstep.

'Nick, what are you doing here?' she asked as she swung open the door.

'Were you in bed?' he asked. His eyes flicked over her nightwear, then rested on her face, which seemed flushed, her eyes wide and bright.

'No…I was just lounging around, watching TV.' Another white lie, she thought grimly. But she wanted Nick to come in, and if she told him she was in bed he'd politely rush away.

'I've just had your mother on the phone,' Nick muttered, stepping past her into the hallway before she could invite him in.

'My mother!' Kate stared at him in astonishment. 'I was just speaking to her a while ago. Why was she phoning you?'

'She's most concerned because she's been trying to phone you for over an hour and there's no answer. She seems to think Stephen might be round here, making a nuisance of himself.'

'Oh, honestly!' Kate rolled her eyes. 'How ridiculous. And what does she think you are going to do about it?' she asked furiously. 'Throw him out on his ear?'

'She just wants to make sure you're OK.' Nick didn't look amused.

'Well, as you can see, I'm fine,' Kate mumbled.

'Good. Give your mother a ring and tell her that.' Nick's eyes darted past her towards the light spilling out from her bedroom. 'How come you're not answering your phone, anyway?'

'I've unplugged it.' Kate shook her head, her eyes blazing. 'I can't get over the fact that my mother rang you! Talk about Big Brother watching me.'

'Yeah, well, Big Brother isn't all that interested in your romantic dalliances, believe me,' Nick grated dryly. 'If you want to go and make a fool of yourself over Stephen, that's your business. There's no point losing your rag with me. I only called out of courtesy to your mother. Nothing else.'

'I'm not making a fool of myself with anybody…what are you talking about, Nick?' Kate frowned. 'Look, I'm really sorry you've been dragged around here on a wild-goose chase. I'm not annoyed with you—'

'Aren't you? Well, I'm annoyed with you,' Nick muttered.

'Are you?' She stared at him, perplexed. 'Why? What have I done?'

'You're standing there pontificating on the fact that your mother is sticking her nose into your affairs and yet you did the very same to me just a few hours ago.'

'When?' Kate shook her head. 'You've lost me totally now.'

'The name Jan doesn't ring any bells, then?' Nick asked sardonically.

'Oh!' Kate closed the front door.

'In all honesty, I could have done without the match-making bit, Kate,' he said irritably. 'You really put me on the spot.'

So that was why he was sounding so annoyed. She felt herself relax. 'Did you and Jan not hit it off, then?' she asked curiously. 'I thought you liked her.'

'That's not the point.'

'It was just coffee, Nick, no big deal.' Suddenly she was light-hearted. 'And you need to start dating again—'

'Do I?' Nick sounded really furious now; his dark eyes blazed into hers.

'Yes, and Jan is nice. She's really good at her job and she's attractive.' Her eyes moved to the front door. 'She's not in the car waiting for you, is she?'

'No, she's not. I dropped her home ages ago.'

'So you didn't get on with her.' Kate shrugged non-chalantly. 'You can't expect to get on with the first person you date after a break-up of a romance. You know the old saying—you have to kiss a few frogs before you find a princess.'

'Very funny.' Nick wasn't laughing. His dark eyes were watchful, intense. 'But I didn't say I didn't get on with her. In fact, we hit it off very well.'

'Oh!'

Kate was momentarily speechless. 'Well, that's really good.' Her voice, when she found it, seemed to have raised a full octave. 'I'm really pleased.'

'Well, I'm pleased that you're pleased,' Nick grated. 'But let this be the last time you try any matchmaking, OK?'

She shrugged helplessly. 'It's no big deal, Nick—'

'It's a big deal to me,' he said seriously. 'Don't do it again.'

'Anybody would think I made a habit of it, the way you're going on,' she muttered crossly. 'And if you've hit it off with Jan, I don't know why you're so annoyed with me.'

'Maybe for the same reason that you were cross a moment ago when you thought I was around here checking up on your private life—'

'I didn't think *you* were checking up on me—'

'Whatever.' He cut across her. 'I can find my own women without any help from you, Kate—'

'I know you can,' Kate retorted, and then grinned at him mischievously. 'Let's just forget about it…shall we? Come on through and I'll make us a cup of tea.'

'No, I won't, thanks. I'll let you get back to your visitor.' His glance went once more towards the hallway.

'What visitor?' Kate stared at him blankly, then realization dawned as she followed his gaze down to her bedroom. 'I'm on my own, Nick! Stephen's gone, remember?' she said sarcastically.

Nick shrugged. 'Of course I remember. But your friends and your mother seem to think his return is imminent.'

'Do they, now?' Kate frowned. 'Have you and Jan been talking about me?'

'Of course we talked about you.' Nick suddenly grinned, his humour restored. His eyes flicked over her, noting the fragile beauty of her features, totally at odds with the fury in her green eyes. 'That's what you get when you throw two of your friends together.'

'Yes, well, you, Jan and my mother, for that matter, can keep your opinions to yourselves. It's none of your business.'

'Now, come on, Katy, we only gossip because we care,' Nick drawled sardonically and was rewarded with an even sharper glare. He held up his hands. 'OK, OK, I get the message,' he agreed with a laugh. 'But don't worry, Jan and I didn't waste too much time talking about you.'

So what had they talked about? Kate wondered, her attention shifting.

'Now we've got all that sorted out, perhaps I will have that cup of tea.' Nick glanced at his watch. 'Do you want me to put the kettle on, while you phone your mother?'

Kate smiled at that. 'Yes…go on, then.'

She returned to her bedroom, plugged the phone back in and dialled her mother's number as she checked her appearance in the dressing-table mirror.

So what actually had happened between Nick and Jan? she wondered. Surely if he was totally smitten he wouldn't have been quite so annoyed with her for introducing them.

She pulled a brush through her hair as she sat at the dressing table, waiting for her call to be answered. She put a dab of perfume behind her ears and at her throat. Then loosened the belt on her white satin dressing gown and unfastened the top button of her nightdress.

Her mother answered the phone. 'Everything's fine, Mum.' She leaned forward and applied a little peach gloss to her lips. Better, she thought. A girl had a certain standard to keep up, she couldn't walk around looking as if she'd just been dragged out of bed…even if she had. 'I unplugged the phone because I wanted to get some sleep. You shouldn't have bothered Nick.'

'Nick didn't mind,' her mother said quickly. 'He's a gentleman, a lovely, lovely man. You know, Kate, you could do worse than set your sights on him. The more I think about it, the more—'

'I've got to go, Mum, he's in my kitchen.'

'Well, if I were you I'd try to keep him there.'

'Lock him in the larder, you mean?' Kate asked with a grin. 'Threaten him with an egg whisk if he tries to leave.'

'You know what I mean.' Her mother refused to see the joke. 'Mind you, I know where you're coming from. Nick is a heartbreaker in a way, doesn't want to settle down. His mother told me that she didn't think he'd ever get married, that he enjoys his freedom too much.'

'Yes, he does,' Kate murmured.

'I just thought that you could use your femininity on him...that you'd be perfect for each other, but you're right, maybe it's not a good idea. You've been disappointed in love enough.'

'Thanks, Mum.'

Honestly, her mother had some crazy notions sometimes; Kate smiled to herself as she put the receiver down. Then she glanced again at her reflection in the mirror. Suddenly she noticed how she had unbuttoned her nightdress, and how provocatively she had arranged her dressing gown to show her figure to its very best advantage. Horrified, she quickly buttoned herself up, then grabbed a tissue and wiped off the lip-gloss. What the hell was she thinking?

'Do you want tea or coffee?' Nick shouted down the hallway.

'Tea.' With a quick glance to reassure her that she was decent, she went out to join him.

'Everything all right?' Nick asked as he took some cups out of a cupboard.

'Fine. I told her not to ring you again, but she didn't pay a blind bit of notice.'

'I don't mind if she phones me.'

'I wouldn't encourage it, if I were you,' Kate muttered as she passed him some milk from the fridge and then sat down at the breakfast bar.

'Why not?'

'Well, she's suddenly got this weird idea that you and I should…' She trailed off in embarrassment as Nick looked over at her.

'Should what?'

Kate shrugged. 'Never mind,' she murmured. 'It's too absurd to even repeat.'

Nick handed her the mug of tea and then sat opposite. 'Go on, tell me,' he urged. 'I could do with a laugh.'

'She thinks…well, you know she's always been your greatest fan.' Kate tried a new tack.

'Yes, of course.' Nick smiled. He watched the colour rise under the delicate creamy skin, highlighting her high cheekbones. Noted how she hid her expressive eyes from him behind the long, dark eyelashes.

She looked delectably attractive. The straight dark, luxuriant hair would have made Cleopatra jealous, and the white silk nightwear seemed to emphasize the honey tan of her skin, the sensual curves of her body, regardless of how tightly they were drawn across her.

'She seems to have this idea in her head that we would be perfect together…'

'We are perfect together.' His smile widened; his eyes gleamed with a spark of amusement. 'The perfect team, we've always got on well.'

She looked over at him, wondering suddenly if he was being deliberately obtuse. He met her eyes innocently, one eyebrow raised.

'For heaven's sake Nick, I'm talking romantically.'

'Romantically?' His grin stretched wider. 'Really?'

'Yes…I told you it was absurd,' she muttered, annoyed

by his smile, by the humour in his tone. 'Even she had to admit it was, once I'd shot her down in flames.'

'Preposterous,' Nick agreed wryly.

'Well, there's no need to be so blunt. I'm not that hideous!'

'I never said you were.' His gaze moved over her thoughtfully, as if she were on display in a shop window with a price on her head. It made her feel intensely self-conscious but, more than that, she was suddenly very aware of the power of his sensuality. There was something almost primal about the way he was weighing her up and it made her body respond with a thrust of adrenalin that was purely sexual.

'In fact, you're not bad-looking at all,' he murmured.

'Well, gee, thanks,' she grated sarcastically.

He grinned again and she realized he was deliberately teasing her.

She took a sip of her tea. 'So, how did your evening go with Jan?' she asked, swiftly changing the subject.

'It was very pleasant; we had dinner at the café. The food's very good in there, you know. They have quite an extensive menu.'

Kate didn't want to hear about the menu. 'And are you going to see her again?'

'We're planning something for next week, after this wedding that you and I are going to.'

'Why aren't you seeing her this week?' Kate asked curiously.

'I'm away on business again tomorrow, and I won't be back until Friday.'

'Oh, I see. But you do like her?' She couldn't seem to leave the subject.

'Yes, I said I did.' Nick finished his tea and put his cup down. 'Do you want me to book that hotel in Stevengar, or are you going to do it?' he asked, his manner suddenly brisk and businesslike.

'I'll do it,' she said easily. 'You're busy, anyway.'

'OK, I'll pick you up on Saturday morning, ten forty-five?'

'Thank you.'

'Don't thank me. Frankly, I think you're crackers to go anywhere near this function,' Nick answered dryly.

'Stephen probably won't even be there.'

Nick slanted her a look of dry disbelief. 'You don't really believe that, do you?'

She shrugged.

'Well, I suppose you know what you're doing.' Nick stood up. 'I'd better go.'

'You know, if you'd rather go with Jan to that party at the weekend, I'll understand.' Kate forced herself to say the words to him as she followed him out towards the front door.

'There'll be other parties,' Nick said nonchalantly. Then glanced around at her with a gleam in his eyes. 'Do you think Jan was the woman you read about in my horoscope? You know, the one I should have met at a party.'

'No.' Kate frowned. 'Because you didn't meet her at a party.'

'Ah, but I might have done if you hadn't dragged her along to the café today.' Nick's smile widened. 'Maybe the forces of fate move in mysterious ways after all, and Jan and I were just destined to meet up, no matter where it was.'

'I don't think so,' Kate murmured, not liking the theory at all.

'Don't you? I am surprised. I thought you were a great believer in destiny and the stars.'

'I am...' Why was her heart going thump, thump

against her chest in that painful way? she wondered. 'But your horoscope said you'd meet someone at a party...not that a friend would introduce you to someone over coffee.' She opened the front door for him.

His eyes travelled over her watchfully. 'I never realized what a precise art star-gazing was,' he drawled laconically.

'Of course it is.' She ignored the humour in his tone. 'Really, you need to have a chart drawn up to have your horoscope properly told.'

Nick put out a hand and angled her chin upwards so that he could look down at her properly. 'So you don't think Jan is my dream woman, then?'

'I didn't say that,' Kate replied, moving out of his reach. The touch of his hand made her skin burn.

He smiled. 'No, you didn't. And, funnily enough, I quite like my theory. Maybe I could be a convert to this mystic stuff after all.'

He watched the flicker of annoyance in her clear green eyes and smiled. 'Goodnight, Katy, sleep well.'

Before she realized his intentions he bent his head and kissed her fully on the lips. It was just a fleeting caress, but it was warm, inviting, and very sensual; it made Kate's senses reel.

Now why did he do that? she wondered dazedly as he walked away from her towards his car.

CHAPTER FIVE

'HAVE you heard anything from Nick?' Jan asked casually as they were finishing work on Friday afternoon.

'No.' Kate glanced across at her colleague. 'Have you?'

'Yes, actually, I spoke to him last night.'

'Oh.' Kate felt a curl of jealousy inside and tried desperately to squash it. 'Well, that's nice,' she said brightly. 'Where is he?'

'Stockholm. But he said to tell you not to worry, he'll be home in time to take you to this wedding.'

'I wasn't worried,' she muttered, slotting some papers into her bag. 'Nick's never let me down.'

'He's like your big brother, isn't he?' Jan said. 'I think it's really sweet.'

'Do you?'

'What was he like when he was young? Have you got any photographs?'

Crikey, Jan had it bad, Kate thought wryly. 'Somewhere, but they are all at my mother's house in London.'

'Shame.' Jan fell into step beside her as they left the office.

'When are you seeing him again?' Kate asked, hoping she didn't sound as nosy as she felt.

'Next Tuesday night...it feels like it's for ever away.'

'It's only a few days...and at least he rang you.'

'What about you, Kate? No news from Stephen yet?' Jan switched the subject quickly.

'No.'

'Never mind.'

I don't mind, actually, Kate thought suddenly. In fact, if I never see Stephen again it will be a day too soon.

'You'll have to start dating again,' Jan continued briskly as they went through the revolving doors out into the sunshine. 'In fact, Nick and I were both saying that yesterday, and I had a brilliant idea.'

Kate slanted a suspicious look at her colleague, wondering what was coming.

'I know a guy you might like. He's called Andre and he's single and I thought—'

'Oh, no!' Kate cut across her immediately.

'Don't be such a stick-in-the-mud. I think you'd like Andre. He's a designer and—'

'Never in a million months of Sundays will I go out on a blind date.'

'Well, Nick seemed to think it was a good idea. He said when you came back from your friend's wedding, that we should organize a foursome and go out to dinner.'

Just wait until I see Nick, Kate thought angrily. And to think that only a few days ago he had dared to tell her off for trying to organize his social life!

'Go on, Kate, it will be fun,' Jan urged again, not one to give in easily. 'He's not bad-looking—'

'So if he's not bad-looking, why haven't you been out with him?' Kate asked crisply.

'I have…but it didn't work out.'

'I'm not going out with him, Jan, so you can stop asking.'

'Just think about it over the weekend,' Jan urged. 'It would be really good fun going out in a foursome.'

Kate tried her best not to think about it as she threw the last of her belongings in her weekend case the next day. Good fun going out in a foursome indeed! She couldn't think of anything worse and when Nick arrived to pick her up she would tell him so in no uncertain manner.

She glanced at the clock. He was due to pick her up soon. They'd decided to travel to the hotel first, check in and change into their wedding outfits.

She checked her appearance again in the bedroom mirror. She'd been to the hairdresser's this morning and had her hair restyled in the latest trendy style. It was just shoulder length now and it bounced with vitality and shine as she turned her head from side to side. The effect was quite stunning.

But even though she looked good, she wasn't particularly confident about attending this wedding. She didn't know whether it was because she was dreading seeing Stephen, or if it was the strange mood that seemed to be hanging over her where Nick was concerned, but, whatever it was, she felt incredibly tense.

Kate slipped into a pair of faded jeans and a cropped top and then carried her overnight bag into the hallway.

The doorbell rang just as she had finished.

Nick did a double take as she opened the door. 'Wow, I like your hair.' He whistled under his breath, admiration in the darkness of his eyes.

'Thanks.' She smiled. Nick was wearing jeans and a T-shirt, but he looked good as well. Healthy, tanned and relaxed, which was more than could be said for herself.

'Have you time for a coffee, or should we get straight off?' she asked as he followed her into the hall.

He glanced at his watch. 'I think we'll hit the road. The traffic might be heavy today—there's a football match on. We can have coffee at the hotel before going to the church, if that's OK with you?' He picked up her bag. 'Crikey, what have you got in here?' he asked wryly. 'The kitchen sink?'

'The wedding present. Don't drop it, it's a clock.'

'What, a grandfather clock?' he teased.

'Ha, ha, very funny.' Kate made a face at him and he laughed.

'You know what, you haven't changed from school, despite the sexy hairstyle.'

'Neither have you, you're still made of puppy dogs' tails.'

'That's why women find me irresistible,' he retorted.

'In your dreams,' she muttered sardonically. 'You're getting too big for your boots, Nick.'

'Well, too big for something…anyway.' He grinned at her cheekily before heading out to the car with her gear.

Honestly, the man was irrepressible. She really would have to have words with Jan, get her to play it cool with him. He needed someone who'd play hard to get. Women fell too easily at his feet. She wondered if that was the reason he got bored and moved on to the next relationship after a short time. There was not enough of a challenge or a chase.

Kate turned to check everything was switched off and then joined him outside.

It was another beautiful day, a clear blue sky and a warm breeze rolling in from the sea.

'Tanya has got a good day for it, anyway,' Nick remarked as he steered the car out towards the main road. 'Have you spoken to her since receiving the invite?'

'Yes, just to accept and ask her what she would like for a wedding present.'

'You didn't ask her if Stephen would be there, then?'

'No.'

He glanced over at her. 'Have you heard from him yet?'

'No and I don't know if I want to,' Kate answered him

truthfully. 'Part of me doesn't want to see him again and the other part...'

'The other part is still in love with him?'

She didn't answer him for a moment. 'I'm not sure what my feelings are for him,' she murmured. 'I'm still very angry with him, I know that. If he wanted to finish with me he should have had the guts to do it properly. I think I deserved to be treated with more respect.'

'Yes, you did.' He glanced sideways at her. She was looking down at her hands now, a pensive look on her features.

'Shall I hit him for you?' Nick cajoled teasingly. 'A quick punch after the church service just so he can't enjoy the food and drink.'

Kate smiled. 'Don't be absurd.'

'Well, at least it brought a smile to your face.'

She grinned. 'What would you have done if I'd accepted the offer?'

'I'd have told you he wasn't worth it.'

'And you're probably right. I suppose I do need to meet someone else,' she said quietly, almost to herself.

'Yes, someone more reliable—'

'And, excuse me, but I don't need you trying to organize blind dates for me,' she rounded on him as she remembered what Jan had told her.

'That's a bit of an irony coming from someone who set me up on a blind date only last week, and didn't even have the courtesy to warn me in advance,' he grated sardonically.

'That wasn't a blind date. It was just a spur of the moment cup of coffee.'

'And this is just a meal,' Nick retorted. 'Apparently Andre is a lovely guy.'

Kate glanced back at him impatiently, and caught the

amused glint in his eye. 'You're enjoying this, aren't you? It's get-your-own-back time for trying to set you up with Jan.'

'Now, what was it you said to me last week...?' Nick grinned. 'Wasn't it something about having to kiss a few frogs before you find your prince?'

'I do wish you wouldn't hang on my every word so, Nick,' she muttered sarcastically and he laughed.

Did Nick really want her to go out with some guy she'd never met? she wondered. Then from nowhere the memory of the way he'd kissed her returned, tormenting and teasing.

Resolutely she pushed the recollection away. That kiss had meant nothing, she told herself fiercely. Nick was her friend and he cared about her, and that was all it was.

'In all honesty, it will be a long time before I want to get seriously involved with a man again,' she said quietly.

Nick glanced over at her, noting the set expression on her face. When Jan had suggested to him that they fix Kate up with a friend of hers, his initial reaction had been very unenthusiastic. But he hadn't tried to talk her out of the idea. Part of him had been curious as to what Kate's reaction would be to the suggestion. Was she ready to start dating again? It seemed the answer to that was no.

They fell silent as he negotiated the heavy traffic. Kate watched the flat countryside as it whizzed past her window. It wasn't very interesting for a while, and then they passed fields of flowers blazing in the midday sun. Windmills dominated the horizon, dark against the pale blue of the sky, reminding her of patterns on the Dutch blue delft.

It was nearing midday as they reached the seaside town of Stevengar. It was a pretty little town, with cobbled streets and quaint old-world buildings. Their hotel was down a long driveway flanked by poplar trees. Kate couldn't see it until they rounded a corner and then its beauty took her aback. It was very old and had obviously once been a very grand castle. There were turrets at both sides and the remains of a moat and a drawbridge that had been turned into a majestic hotel entrance. A mist hung low around the castle walls—it was probably a heat haze coming in from the flat marshland surrounding them, but somehow it lent an air of mystery and romance to the place.

'This hotel was quite a find,' Nick remarked as he parked the car.

'Yes, you're right, but I didn't find it, Tanya did. She's having her reception at the banqueting suites here.'

'It's a lovely setting. I'll have to keep it in mind if I ever tie the knot.'

Kate glanced over at him, quite startled by the remark. Nick never talked about marriage; in fact the very word usually made him turn quite green.

'Are you serious?'

'One day I might be.' He grinned at her and climbed out of the car to get their luggage.

'When pigs are flying and tulips are worth their weight in gold again?'

'Something like that,' he agreed dryly.

Their feet crunched over the gravel as they walked towards the foyer. Kate was momentarily distracted as she looked up at the sheer scale of the stone walls. It was an enormous building, even more impressive close up than at a distance.

The reception was a vast area carpeted in red, a grand curving staircase led down from a gallery that encircled the area, and flowers adorned the large reception desk where a young woman smiled a warm welcome.

There were spectacular stained-glass windows around

the sides of the room and Kate browsed around to admire them as Nick checked in.

She was debating buying a few postcards from a stand near the entrance when a familiar voice spoke behind her.

'Hi, Kate, it's nice to see you again.'

She turned and there was Stephen. It was illogical to feel shocked by his presence here, she'd known that there was a chance of seeing him today, but somehow she hadn't expected it quite so soon and she was totally unprepared for the effect it had on her system.

She felt the colour drain from her face, felt her heart thump against her chest as if it were trying to escape.

'How are you?' he asked gently.

What a hypocrite, she thought suddenly. As if he cared. Her eyes flicked over his good-looking features, disdainfully. 'I'm absolutely fine, Stephen,' she said coolly. She was quite pleased with the sound of her voice because it held no hint of the turmoil inside.

'That's good.' He nodded, then his eyes flicked towards Nick who was standing with his back to them at the reception desk. 'You here with Nick?' he asked.

'It would appear so, wouldn't it?' she murmured, not able to resist sarcasm. 'You here with Natasha?'

'Yes... But I miss you, Kate—'

'Really, well, I don't miss you,' Kate said in a low, cold tone. 'And your stuff is packed and ready for you to collect when you get around to it.' Heavens, that felt good, she thought, suddenly enjoying herself.

'Come on, Kate, don't be like this.' His blue eyes narrowed as if she'd hurt him. 'I still care about you—'

Whatever else he was going to say was cut short when Nick walked across towards them.

'Hello, Nick.' Stephen smiled at him, a hint of uncertainty and nervousness about his manner now.

Nick acknowledged the other man with a cool nod. Then turned his attention to Kate. 'We're checked in.' He put his arm around her waist and his voice lowered huskily. 'Shall we go upstairs, or would you like a drink in the bar?'

Something about the way he said those words and looked into her eyes made Kate feel hot inside.

'No…we'll go straight upstairs, shall we?' she murmured.

She was conscious of Stephen watching them as they walked towards the lifts. Nick kept his arm lightly around her waist, and she had to admit she liked the feeling it gave her.

'Are you OK?' he asked once the doors had closed on the foyer, and Stephen.

'Yes.' She leaned back against the mirrored walls wishing Nick hadn't moved his arm away as soon as they were alone.

'I told you this was a mistake,' Nick muttered grimly as he took in the pallor of her skin.

'A good friend isn't supposed to say, I told you so,' Kate murmured, and then smiled at him with a return of her old spirit. 'And, anyway, I handled myself all right out there. Told Stephen to come and pick up his stuff.'

'What did he say to you?'

'That he missed me.' She frowned. 'I wonder what's behind those words, what he's really thinking?'

Nick shrugged. 'I couldn't give a damn what Stephen is thinking and neither should you.'

'I know you're right.'

'But you still do.' Nick met her eyes with a dark, impatient gaze.

'Not in the way you mean,' Kate said firmly. 'I'm not

falling to pieces, Nick.' She angled her chin up, a determinedly stubborn look on her beautiful face.

Nick smiled at her. 'You're gorgeous when you're angry, do you know that?' he said suddenly.

The words threw a jolt of pure pleasure through her body. But there was also something else: a strong feeling of sensuality seemed to spark between them for just an instant. Like an electric current it sizzled in the air and then the lift doors swished open, breaking the sudden tension.

Was that in my imagination? Kate wondered dazedly as Nick broke eye contact and led the way out of the lift.

'Nick?'

He looked around at her, in an almost distracted way. 'Yes?'

It must have been her imagination. He was thinking about something else now, his eyes held a faraway expression. She shrugged, feeling foolish. 'Nothing...'

She watched as he pushed a security card into a bedroom door and opened it. Then they walked into a large and very luxurious suite. The Persian carpets were palest gold, and the furniture rivalled anything out of a stately home.

'I'm sure this isn't what I booked.' Perplexed, Kate wandered past the blue settees towards the window.

The view was spectacular. They could see for miles over the sweep of a golden beach and the sea.

'Don't you like it?' Nick asked.

'It's fabulous.' Kate glanced around; two doors led off the room. She opened one that led through to a massive bedroom with a four-poster bed. 'But I didn't request a suite.'

'I did. I upgraded when I was at Reception,' Nick replied nonchalantly.

'Wow!' She stepped through the doorway and sat down on the side of the four-poster bed. 'This is great—where are you going to sleep?'

'You mean I can't stay in here?' he asked teasingly.

Kate wished he wouldn't look at her like that, with those incredibly sexy eyes. She could feel herself melt inside like an ice cream in the Tropics. 'No, sorry,' she said breezily, 'but I'm commandeering this bed.'

'Pity...' Nick drawled. 'Such a romantic room seems wasted just on one.'

She knew he was teasing her, could recognise his sense of humour after all these years. And yet perversely she wished he weren't. A feeling of regret hit her out of nowhere and it confused her, irritated her.

Where were these sudden feelings for Nick coming from? Something wasn't right. Her emotions were totally in chaos. Which was strange because, apart from the initial shock of seeing Stephen, she had thought that her emotions were in pretty good shape.

'Well, you never know,' she said airily, trying to cover a sudden feeling of embarrassment. 'Maybe Mr Wonderful will be at the wedding and I'll fall into his arms later.'

'Oh, no!' Nick shook his head. 'You're saving yourself for Andre next week. And meanwhile I'm camping outside your door.'

Kate smiled at him, but despite the tilt of her head, the spark in her eyes, there was something vulnerable about the smile. 'You've no need to worry, Nick,' she said quietly. 'I can assure you I was only joking. As I told you in the car, I'm off men at the moment. So standing guard outside my door would be a complete waste of time.'

All eyes were centred on the bride and groom in the small chapel. They pledged their vows, in clear voices, gazing with love into each other's eyes. Tanya looked beautiful. Her dress was a delicate ivory; it fitted in to her tiny waist and fell to the floor in yards of silk. David was the perfect foil for her blonde beauty in his dark suit.

Kate watched the ceremony with a tear in her eye. It was such a joyful occasion and yet so serious that it was impossible not to feel moved by it.

Nick's attention wandered from the ceremony to Kate. She looked radiantly beautiful in the buttercup-yellow suit, a wide-brimmed straw hat tilted at a becoming angle. She really was a very beautiful woman, he thought. She had always been attractive and as a child she had been cute. But now she was just gorgeous.

He watched as she got a tissue out of her bag and dabbed it at her eyes. She caught his gaze and smiled, a wistful, tremulous kind of smile, which tugged at his emotions for some reason.

'I love to cry at weddings,' she whispered.

Was she thinking about Stephen? he wondered suddenly as she turned her attention back to the ceremony. Was she wishing that had been them, standing up there taking their vows?

For a moment he felt raw anger towards the other man, who was sitting several rows behind them. He'd never liked Stephen. There had been times when he'd let her down, and Nick had desperately wanted to say something to him, even if it was only, Get your act together. But for the sake of his friendship with Kate he'd bitten his tongue. She had loved Stephen and he'd had to respect that, but it had taken all his self-control. Even today when he'd seen Stephen talking to her in the foyer he'd wanted to go over there and tell him exactly what he thought of him. But he had to tread warily. If they did get back together again, that would leave his friendship with Kate in a tenuous situation.

The notion that they might get back together appalled him. But he couldn't rule out the possibility. According to Jan, Kate was even more devastated about the split than she was letting on. And with Stephen having the audacity to tell her he missed her, it was obvious the guy was hedging his bets. The prospect of Kate falling for a sob story or a few charming lines and taking him back made Nick's hands clench into tight fists at his side.

Nick tried to turn his thoughts back to the wedding and close it out. Kate was an intelligent woman; she knew what she was doing. She wouldn't have Stephen back. She just needed time to adjust, and in the meantime he intended to be there for her.

As the happy couple walked back down the aisle hand in hand everyone filed out of the church behind them. The sunshine was blinding and the bells pealed out merrily into the warmth of the summer afternoon as confetti was thrown and pictures were taken.

There were a lot of people in the churchyard and it wasn't until the crowds started to thin out that Kate noticed Stephen with Natasha for the first time.

Natasha was wearing a pale blue suit, her blonde hair swept up in a sophisticated style. Stephen was wearing a dark suit and a blue tie, which was one, unless she was very much mistaken, that she had given him last Christmas. Who would have thought that less than eight months later he'd be wearing it while out with another woman? she found herself thinking wryly. Life was very strange sometimes.

Stephen glanced over and their eyes met across the pathway. He smiled at her, but it was a smile she didn't bother to return.

'Shall we go on to the reception?' Nick put a hand on her arm and she looked up at him.

'Yes, let's get out of here,' she said.

'It was a lovely service, don't you think?' she said brightly, trying to turn her mind away from Stephen as they walked back towards the car park. 'Very enjoyable.'

'Really?' Nick flicked a dry gaze at her.

'What's the matter? Why are you looking at me like that?'

'Just that I didn't think you were enjoying yourself at all. You were crying.'

'I always cry at weddings; I find them very moving.'

'You didn't cry at my cousin Sandra's wedding last year.'

'I did!'

'Well, I don't remember.'

'Probably because you were too busy admiring the blonde bridesmaid.'

Nick laughed at that.

'What did you think of Natasha, by the way?' Kate couldn't help herself from asking curiously as they climbed into his car.

'Never noticed her,' Nick said grimly.

'You must have noticed her.'

'Why? Just because you can't tear your eyes away from Stephen, doesn't mean everyone is as fixated.'

'I'm not fixated.'

'Aren't you? You could have fooled me.'

Kate was hurt by the blunt words. 'Nick, you can't expect me to just forget him instantly. It's normal to be curious about him, about the other woman in his life now.'

Nick didn't reply. He started up the car engine.

'Don't you ever think about Serena?' Kate asked him suddenly.

Nick shrugged. 'Occasionally. But I wasn't in love with Serena.'

Was I in love with Stephen? Kate wondered suddenly. She had used to think that she was, wouldn't have moved in with him otherwise. But today when she had looked across at him in that churchyard, it had been like looking at a total stranger. Could real love die that quickly?

She glanced over at Nick. He looked very handsome in his dark suit. She allowed her gaze to move over his profile, studying him. If Nick never spoke to her again, if she couldn't see him, she would be devastated. Yet, Stephen hadn't devastated her. Dented her pride, yes, hurt her, yes, but as for anything deeper...she really didn't know. In fact she felt a bit numb inside sometimes, as if the person who had lived with Stephen had been someone else. As if she were outside herself now, looking in. It was the weirdest feeling. Maybe it was just shock.

Nick pulled the car to a standstill back at the Castle Hotel. For a while they both just sat there, watching as other guests from the wedding pulled up and went inside.

Then they saw Stephen arrive. He was sitting in the passenger side of a red sports car. Natasha was driving.

'How do you want to play this?' Nick asked Kate suddenly, looking over at her. 'Am I your best friend, or your lover?'

The question startled her. For a second she couldn't answer.

He tipped his head to one side, a gleam of amusement in his eyes. 'I can do either, quite well.'

'I know.' She smiled tremulously. 'Well, I know you can do the best-friend bit...' she added hastily, her cheeks suddenly starting to glow pink. 'I'll have to take your word for the other.'

He reached across and brushed a stray strand of her

hair away from her face. The gesture was curiously
tender; it made her heart speed up, and it made her body
ache with some kind of emotion she really couldn't place.

'Were you thinking about Stephen in church today?'

'Not really.' Kate could tell he didn't believe her. 'I
mean, I suppose it's normal to think back on your own
relationship when you attend a wedding, but it was a fleeting thing. I wasn't dwelling on it.'

'So the tears weren't for him?'

'No!' She glared at him fiercely, 'Certainly not. I told
you, weddings just make me emotional.' She wondered
suddenly what he would say if she told him that she was
starting to suspect that Stephen hadn't broken her heart.
And that she must never really have loved him…or at
least not loved him enough. Would he be shocked? She
had to admit that she was shocked at the observation herself. But how else could she explain the fact that she had
looked at Stephen across that churchyard today and felt
as if she were looking at a stranger?

Nick watched the clouds of uncertainty pass over
Kate's features. 'Do you know what I thought when I sat
in church today?' he asked gently. 'I thought how beautiful you were.'

She smiled at that. 'Flattery will get you everywhere.'

'Now, if only that were true,' he teased.

For a moment there was silence. Kate stared into his
eyes and found herself wishing that he weren't joking.

'Anyway…' She dragged her gaze away from his. 'I
wasn't upset about Stephen today,' she said firmly.

Nick glanced past her and watched for a moment as
Natasha made several attempts to back her car into a small
space at the other side of the car park.

'So you don't want to give him something to think
about, then?'

Kate shrugged. 'I told you before, Stephen would never believe we were having an affair,' she murmured. 'He knows us...knows our history.'

'And I told you, I think I could put up quite a persuasive act.'

She remembered the last time he had said that, then the way he had kissed her, and she felt her heartbeats increase dramatically.

'Maybe trying to fake a grand passion is being a bit optimistic anyway.' She tried desperately to sound sensible and in control. 'As everyone knows we've always been just friends, we might do best to feign a budding romance. Just an arm around my shoulder and a special smile now and then.'

'Perhaps you'd like to write me a script?' Nick asked sardonically.

'I think we'll just work the "least said, soonest mended" approach—' Kate broke off in mid-sentence as he leaned closer towards her.

'What are you doing?' she asked him in panic.

'I'm working the "least said" approach,' he murmured with a gleam of devilment in his eye. He leaned further across and kissed her on the lips. The gentleness of the caress took her breath away. She felt herself lose all sense of reality; the minutes ticked by and she felt she was drowning in a sea of emotion. Nobody had ever stirred her senses so completely just with a kiss. She felt her whole body heat up, her lips tingle, and her senses reel with latent desire. She wanted him in those few seconds and the need was quite startlingly vehement.

When he released her she was totally dazed. He smiled, his face still just inches from hers. 'Has anyone ever told you that you are a good kisser?' he said huskily.

Kate could hardly find her breath to answer that.

'I...don't think so.' She cringed at the tremulous tone of her own voice; she sounded as shaken as she felt.

Nick's glance moved past her out of the window. 'I think that should just about have done it.'

'Done what?'

'Given Stephen something to think about.'

The matter-of-fact words brought Kate back to reality with a thump. She pulled back from him and looked out of the window. Stephen and Natasha had just walked past their car.

She didn't have time to say anything else because Nick was already climbing out.

This wasn't a good idea, Kate thought, feeling suddenly panic-stricken as she watched Nick walk around to open the passenger door for her, a look of determination in his eyes. Obviously he had warmed to the idea of this charade; he'd never liked Stephen and he'd decided he was going to enjoy making it clear the other man was no longer wanted. But perversely Kate was now remembering his words of caution when she had suggested this. 'Toying with emotions is always dangerous,' he had said.

How right he was, she thought now as she stepped out of the car and he reached to take hold of her hand. But it wasn't Stephen's emotions she was thinking about. It was her own.

CHAPTER SIX

THE large banqueting suite was filled to capacity. Kate and Nick found themselves seated at the end of one of the large trestle tables surrounded by a group of Tanya's friends that Kate didn't know very well.

'Jez Tailor.' The guy seated next to her supplied his name as she strove to remember it. 'We met at Tanya's birthday party last year.'

'Oh, yes.' Kate smiled at him. 'I'm—'

'Kate Murray.' He finished for her with a grin.

Her eyes widened. 'You've got a good memory.'

'For a pretty face, I have.'

She could have done without the charm, Kate thought. But he seemed pleasant enough. Probably about her age, his eyes were hazel, his hair was light brown, and he'd a nice smile.

'Last time I saw you, you were with your partner...now what was his name?'

'Stephen. We've split up.'

'I've split up from my partner since then as well,' the man informed her.

As the food was served he proceeded to tell her all about it.

Across the table she met Nick's laconic gaze. Obviously he wasn't impressed with Jez Tailor, Kate thought wryly.

She watched surreptitiously as the woman next to him engaged him in conversation. She was a very attractive blonde, probably a little older than Nick. Kate watched how she lit up when Nick smiled at her, and then leaned further towards him, ignoring the man on her other side.

Nick had quite a lethal effect on women, she thought dryly. He seemed to exert a hypnotic spell over them without even being aware that he was doing it.

Kate accepted another glass of champagne, listening with half an ear to Jez as he went into the lurid details of his relationship breakdown.

It was a relief when the speeches started and Kate could sit back and listen to some amusing and happy anecdotes.

Then everyone stood up as the room was prepared for the evening party. Across the crowds, Kate caught sight of Stephen. She had noticed that Tanya had seated him at the other end of the room from her and she was grateful for that. She just hoped that their paths wouldn't cross too much in the next few hours, because she wasn't sure if she was really up to it.

Nick found a quiet seat next to the windows overlooking the floodlit garden. 'Would you like a drink?'

Kate glanced across towards the crowd at the bar, one of which was Stephen.

'No, thanks, I'm OK for now.'

Nick sat down, stretching his legs out. 'I'm glad we've lost your admirer, he was starting to give me a headache.'

'Who?' Kate gave up her attempt to surreptitiously watch Stephen.

'Jez,' Nick said flatly, his eyes narrowing slightly, making her guiltily aware that he knew very well where her attention had just been. 'He seemed to have it pretty bad for you.'

'I think he's just lonely. Poor guy has gone through a terrible break-up.'

'Yes, so I heard,' Nick said dryly. 'In fact I think the whole table heard.'

'Actually, I think the table were more interested in watching that woman sitting next to you, trying to devour you for dessert,' Kate couldn't resist retorting.

'At least she was entertaining.'

For some reason the gleam of male approval in his voice for the other woman irritated Kate. 'Sometimes you are really horrible, Nick,' she snapped. 'Jez just needed a sympathetic person to talk to, that's what it's like when you've got a broken heart. But as you've never in your life been ditched I don't suppose you'd know that.'

'Hey!' Nick leaned forward and she suddenly found that his face was just a few inches apart from hers. 'Why are you having a go at me?'

'I'm not having a go at you,' she backtracked swiftly, aware that she had indeed been having a dig at him. She couldn't even understand why.

'Certainly sounded like it.'

For a second she looked into his eyes and felt her heart skip unevenly. 'Just try and be a bit more sympathetic,' she said bleakly. 'OK?'

'I don't know why you're so defensive, you don't even know the guy that well,' Nick muttered, leaning back in his chair again. 'And if you want to know the truth, I don't think he really remembered your name,' he added. 'He was reading your place card.'

'One of your tricks, I suppose?'

He shrugged, a hint of amusement in his eyes.

'You're incorrigible, Nick.' Kate had to laugh.

'That's better,' Nick said gently. 'We're supposed to be in love, remember?'

She felt her heart miss a beat at those quietly spoken words and the way he looked at her.

A band was starting to tune up on the raised platform

at the other side of the room and someone dimmed the lights.

A waiter came around with a tray of champagne. Nick handed her a glass. 'Let's relax and enjoy ourselves,' he said huskily.

What would it be like to have Nick as a boyfriend? she wondered suddenly. What would it be like to sit here with him, and know that later he would make love to her upstairs in that four-poster bed? Kate was glad that the lights had dimmed as she felt her pulses racing into total disarray.

She glanced across at him, secretly studying him. He was almost too good-looking, she thought. And there was something wildly exciting about the way he met her eyes sometimes, or smiled in that certain, teasing way of his. What would happen if she started to flirt with him, tried to seduce him?

The notion taunted her playfully, heating her senses. Then reality hit hard. She must be mad to even contemplate such a thing, because all it would do was jeopardize a wonderful friendship and for what—a roll in the sack...or if she was lucky a brief affair? But if she was hoping for anything else she would be kidding herself. Just as all the other women in Nick's life had kidded themselves. So thoughts like these were totally pointless.

She wrenched her eyes away from Nick as the music struck up and the bride and groom took to the floor for the first dance.

That was true love, Kate thought wistfully. One day maybe she would have that. But at the moment it seemed very, very far away.

The music changed and the band played another slow ballad as more couples joined the bride and groom on the floor.

'Shall we dance?' Nick asked. Before she could reply he took the glass of champagne from her and put it down. Then he caught hold of her hand and led her out amongst the crowd.

For a moment Kate stood uncomfortably apart from him. She'd been at discos with Nick before, but she'd never had a slow dance with him and she felt kind of awkward about moving into the circle of his arms, especially after the direction her thoughts had just been taking.

Someone jostled against her and Nick reached out, his arms going around her as if it was the most natural thing in the world. For a second she was tense, trying to hold herself away from his body, then he drew her gently closer, and she was enveloped in his warmth, in his tenderness. She leaned her head against his chest and allowed herself to relax. The feeling was hedonistically blissful.

The touch of his hand against her back, the feel of his body pressed closely against hers made her senses stir. This was where she belonged, she thought dreamily. This just felt right.

The music changed to another slow song and they continued to move with the rhythm. Kate wound her arms further up around his shoulders.

She felt blissfully unaware of her surroundings, of everything except Nick and the feel of his body pressed close against hers, until somebody bumped into her and she was jolted out of her reverie.

She pulled back from Nick and looked up at him, her heart thundering against her chest.

'Shall we go and have another drink?' he asked gently.

Kate wanted to say no, she wanted to say that she'd just like to go back into his arms, but she forced herself to pull away from him. 'Good idea.'

She got separated from Nick as Tanya detained her by the edge of the dance-floor.

'It's been a wonderful day, Tanya.'

Tanya nodded. 'I've enjoyed every minute of it,' she sighed happily. 'And David is whisking me off to the Caribbean on honeymoon tomorrow.' She put a finger over her lips. 'But I'm not supposed to know,' she whispered.

Kate laughed.

'Now, what's the low-down with you and Nick?' Tanya asked curiously. 'Stephen tells me he saw you kissing?'

'Did he?' Kate shrugged. 'Well, it's really none of Stephen's business any more.'

'No, it's not,' Tanya agreed, and then leaned forward with a sparkle of mischief in her eyes. 'But if you are trying to get him jealous, it's working. He's eaten alive with it.'

'I couldn't care less how Stephen feels,' Kate murmured honestly.

'Good for you.' Tanya smiled. 'And I think Nick is gorgeous.'

'So do I.' Kate looked around for him and spotted him by the bar talking to the woman who had sat next to him during the meal. As she watched she saw the woman writing something down on a beer mat, handing it to him with a smile. It was probably her telephone number, Kate thought, and the thrust of jealousy that sliced through her was so intense that it was shocking.

'See you later, Kate.' Tanya rushed off to speak to someone else and Kate was left standing by the edge of the dance-floor feeling slightly sick.

I'm in love with Nick, she thought suddenly. I'm absolutely crazy about him. The realization hit her out of nowhere, totally incapacitating her. All she could do was stand and stare across the crowds at him. What an idiot, she thought. Why hadn't she realized before now just how much he meant to her?

'Hello, Kate.'

She heard Stephen's voice as if it were coming from a distance and glanced around at him blankly. 'Oh, hi.' Her voice sounded as distracted as she felt.

'Listen, Kate, I'm really sorry the way things have worked out.' Stephen's tone was suddenly urgent. 'Do you think we could talk? I need to work through a few things and I'd like to explain—'

'Please don't, Stephen.' She cut across him firmly, before he could continue.

'But I need to. I've been doing a lot of thinking—wondering where things went wrong between us—'

'I think the grey area was called Natasha, wasn't it?' Kate couldn't resist the sarcastic retort.

Stephen shook his head. 'I think Natasha was a panic attack. I knew you'd want me to make a commitment and I wasn't ready for it—'

'That's just rubbish, Stephen, and you know it. But I think maybe you've done me a favour leaving, because I realize now that things could never have worked out between us.'

'You don't mean that!'

'I'm afraid I do.'

'Is it because of Nick?' Stephen's voice hardened, his eyes narrowed. 'I've always known you had a thing for him.'

'No, I haven't. My feelings for him were unexpected and very recent—'

'Oh, come on, Kate. Don't try and kid a kidder. I can see straight through it. I always said that a man and a woman could never be just good friends.'

'Yes, they can. And it's none of your business now, anyway,' Kate said crossly. 'Just leave me alone, Stephen.'

'You won't get him to settle down, you know,' Stephen said suddenly. 'The guy is more afraid of commitment than I am, and that's saying something.'

'Maybe I don't want to settle down,' Kate snapped.

'Of course you do. You want a family and—'

'Look, Stephen, I don't want to discuss this with you. Shouldn't you be getting back to Natasha?'

'Can I come around to the apartment next week and see you?' Stephen asked, totally ignoring her.

'No—'

'I'll take you for dinner to that little restaurant you like so much.'

'No, Stephen—'

'Seven o clock next Tuesday, how's that?'

Kate shook her head. 'I can't.'

'Course you can. We've got unfinished business, Kate.' He smiled at her in that gentle way she remembered so well. For some reason it made her feel sad.

'You did care about me once, Kate, and I let you down, I know that.' He reached out a hand and touched her face. 'But I swear I've learnt my lesson and I won't do it again if you give me another chance.'

'Stephen—'

He put his finger over her lips before she could say anything else. 'Just think about it…about the way things used to be between us. I'll call you…'

Then he was gone, melting into the crowds. Kate forced herself to move in the opposite direction. All of a sudden she just wanted to get out of here. Her emotions were in chaos; it was too hot and stuffy to even think.

The relief when she got out into the reception area was

immense. It was so quiet and cool. Without stopping, she continued through towards the lifts. One was sitting open and empty and she stepped inside and pressed the button for her floor.

Stephen was right, she thought wryly as she watched the lights flick through the different floors. Nick didn't want commitment. Falling for him was asking for heartache, besides which he was her friend. If she had an affair with him she had more to lose than she had to gain.

You're not really in love with him, she told herself over and over again. You're just in a fragile state of mind because of Stephen.

The doors of the lift opened on her floor and Kate walked slowly towards her room, her mind still preoccupied with thoughts of Nick.

It wasn't until she was outside the door to her suite that she realized that she didn't have a card to get in.

She was about to go back downstairs when the lift doors opened again and Nick walked out.

Just the sight of him made her heart thump uncomfortably against her chest.

'Looking for this?' he asked, holding up one of the security plastic cards.

'Yes, I was.' Kate couldn't bring herself to look him in the eye. Just say he could read what was there? Just say he found out how she felt about him? The embarrassment would kill her. But, more than that, it would be the end of their friendship. How could it continue if he found out? It would be an impossible situation.

Nick walked towards her and, inserting the card, opened the door for her. 'So how come you were sneaking away without saying anything?'

'I wasn't sneaking away...I just needed some space,

that's all.' Her voice was very defensive. 'You can go back to the party now.'

He didn't make any reply to that; instead he stepped into the room behind her.

'So what did lover boy say to make you rush off so quickly?' he asked drolly as he watched her take off the jacket of her suit and go across to the mini bar to pour a large glass of Coke.

'You saw him, then?' Kate stalled for time. Her hand shook a little and the drink spilled onto the polished wood surface.

'Obviously.'

'He wants to take me out for dinner next week.' She spoke without looking at him. 'He says he wants a chance to explain why he left. That he wasn't thinking clearly.'

'You can say that again.' Nick snorted derisively. 'The guy's a jerk. You're not going to fall for that, are you?'

'I don't know what I'm going to do,' Kate answered honestly. But she wasn't talking about Stephen now. Stephen was history; she would never go back with him.

'For heaven's sake, Kate, open your eyes. The only person Stephen loves is himself. He only wants you back now because he thinks he can't have you.'

'Well, thanks for the vote of confidence.' She glared at him. 'Why don't you just go back downstairs to your groupie and leave me in peace?'

'My groupie?' Nick looked thoroughly amused for a second.

'The blonde who was writing down her telephone number for you.'

Nick shrugged.

'You're no angel yourself, Nick, so get off Stephen's back.'

'I never said I was an angel,' he answered coolly.

'No, you didn't.' Kate looked down at the drink in her hand and was horrified to find her eyes filling with tears.

'Hey!' Nick's voice was suddenly gentle and he came towards her. 'Don't let Stephen upset you.'

'I'm not.' She glared at the glass of Coke, trying desperately to pull herself together.

'Yes, you are.' He took the glass off her and put it down, his manner firm. Then he tipped her face up towards his. The touch of his hands against her skin made her want to melt. 'He's not worth it, Kate.'

'So you keep telling me.' Her lips twisted wryly. She wondered what he'd think if he knew what she'd really been upset about. That she imagined herself in love with him.

He'd probably think it was amusing…to start with, anyway. Then what would happen?

Kate looked up into the darkness of his eyes. She wanted him to kiss her, wanted to fold herself into his arms and ask him to make love to her.

She pulled away from the touch of his hands in panic and blinked her tears away furiously.

'I know this hurts, Kate, but I don't think Stephen has ever really loved you, and if you go back to him you'll be settling for second best.'

'I've no intention of settling for second best,' Kate said crossly. 'In fact, I'm seriously thinking that it might be OK to never settle for anything. Concentrate on my career and give men up permanently.'

'Don't be ridiculous.' There was a glint of amusement in Nick's tone now. 'You're not cut out to be a nun, Kate.'

'How do you know?' She angled her head up and met his eye with resolve.

'Because I'm a man and I know these things.' He grinned.

'You don't know everything.'

'Well, put it this way, it took me one kiss to figure out that you'd never make a nun.'

'Don't…don't be absurd!'

Nick looked over at her, watched the way her breasts moved under the tight confines of her scoop-necked top as if she was having difficulty controlling her breathing.

'You think I'm being absurd,' he murmured quietly. 'Come here.'

She took a step backwards. 'Why?'

'Because I want to prove to you that there's no way on God's green earth that you can become a nun.'

'I…I'd rather you didn't.' Her chest suddenly felt tight, her skin hot.

'What's the matter? Frightened that I'm going to prove you wrong?'

'No!'

Nick caught her by the arm as she made to move further away from him.

'You are a passionate woman. Katy, you proved that when you kissed me today.'

'I was acting when I kissed you,' she said, trying to keep her voice cool and steady. 'It was for Stephen's benefit, nothing else.'

'Really?' The amusement wasn't quite so noticeable in his voice now.

She wondered if that remark had dented his ego. In a way, she hoped it had, he was too sure of himself sometimes.

'Shall we put your acting abilities to the test again, then?' he asked softly. 'Now that Stephen isn't here.'

Nervously she told herself that she should pull away. But would one quick kiss do any harm? It might be a disappointment. She might be imagining all these feelings clamouring inside.

His eyes moved to her lips and she felt herself quake under the dark, disturbing intensity of his gaze. Maybe it wasn't in her imagination, she acknowledged uneasily. And if that was the case and he kissed her again she was sure she wouldn't be able to keep up any cool pretence. She would respond wholeheartedly, in a manner that would totally dispute all her brave words feigning indifference.

'Nick, I don't think this is a good idea...'

Those panicky words were the last coherent ones that Kate spoke. As his lips met hers she felt a wild exhilaration thrill through her and rational thought was lost.

His lips teased her lightly at first, then as she responded they moved with a slow kind of drugging ecstasy over hers.

Then he was kissing her face, her cheeks, the side of her neck, his arms drawing her tightly against his body. The effect was far more lethal than it had been in the car, or the other night.

She felt delicious little shudders of pleasure shoot through her as she felt his hands moving over her back, pulling up the silk top until he found her skin underneath, his fingers spreading over its softness, curving around her tiny waist before massaging and exploring higher.

'I've been wanting to do this for a long time,' he breathed against her ear.

The words were like fuel to a raging fire. She found his lips and kissed him hungrily.

His hands moved around, cupping the sides of her body, his thumbs stroking over her ribcage, tantalizingly, provocatively, so that her breasts ached for him to move higher and touch her more intimately.

The shrill ring of the telephone cut through the room. The sound made them break guiltily apart.

For a second they just stared at each other, wordlessly, while the phone rang and rang. Neither made any attempt to go and answer it.

'If that was acting, Kate, you're a hell of an actress,' Nick murmured huskily, his eyes narrowed on her face.

The phone stopped ringing. In the silence between them Kate could hear her heart beating in her ears.

'I wasn't acting,' she said softly, giving up all pretence.

He smiled, a teasing, seductive smile that tore at her heart. Then reached out a hand to pull her back into his arms, a purposeful look in his eyes that only served to inflame her senses more. She wanted him so much that she felt the ache of longing eating her up inside.

His hands stroked over the soft shape of her body through the silk top, touching her nipples and gently arousing her with just the lightest pressure of his fingers.

Then he was undressing her, unbuttoning her top and discarding it with ease. His hand moved to the zip of her skirt and it too slithered to the floor until she stood before him in just lacy bra and pants.

It felt wildly wicked to stand and allow him to undress her but the sensation was so erotic that she couldn't pull back, didn't want to think about consequences, didn't want to think about anything except the touch of his hands and the way he was looking at her.

She swallowed hard as Nick kissed her again. The kiss was sensual, invading every part of her mind, his hands running over the lace of her bra, touching her through the glossy material in a way that made her senses clamour for more.

Kate reached up and put her arms around him, kissing

him back with fierce need as he picked her up and carried her towards the bedroom.

As he laid her down on the bed he unfastened her bra, then her matching lacy panties were discarded as he quickly started to divest himself of his own clothing. Nick had a fabulous body, she thought hazily. Powerful shoulders and arms, a wide, strong chest that tapered down towards a very flat, tightly muscled stomach.

She felt her heart flip crazily as he joined her in the deep comfort of the double bed.

'Now where were we?' he murmured provocatively as he looked into her eyes. His hands moved to cup the heaviness of her naked breasts, his fingers teasing the delicate peaks with infinite care. The sensation was wildly erotic, she didn't think it was possible to be any more turned on than she was, and then his lips moved to replace his fingers, causing a torrent of sweet, seductive torment to overpower her senses completely.

She raked her fingers through the softness of his hair, her eyes closed, her breathing ragged. His hands stroked up over her body, finding the soft core of her womanhood, stroking her to a breathless frenzy of desire, then his lips covered her own as he moved on top of her. She felt the full force of his powerful body, naked skin pressed against naked skin. Her hands raked down his back, she murmured incoherently for him to possess her, for him to give her release from the pent-up longing that screamed inside with the need for him to possess her totally.

'Patience,' he whispered softly against her ear, nibbling gently, teasing her even more as his body toyed provocatively with her.

'I need you, Nick.' She whispered the words urgently. Then she felt him inside her and the ecstasy was almost more than she could bear; she was hanging onto control by a whisper.

His body moved slowly against hers at first, commanding and controlling her, his fingers stroking her breasts at the same time. She stretched up her arms, holding onto the bedpost behind.

'Katy, you're so beautiful.' Nick's lips were hungry against hers, his hands fervent as they stroked over her naked body. And then they were both spiralling out of control and into total blissful release.

CHAPTER SEVEN

KATE awoke in darkness entwined in Nick's arms and just lay savouring the feeling. He was asleep, she could hear the steady beat of his heart against her ear, feel the satin smoothness of his skin pressed against hers. His body, so strong and powerful, curved around her so tenderly and protectively.

She had always suspected that Nick would be a fabulous lover, but she had never in her wildest moments expected to feel such exquisite pleasure...or such deep love. Never had she felt so close to anyone, so cherished, so totally sated.

If someone were to grant her a wish now, she would wish that she could wake up every morning like this, with Nick next to her. Was that wishing for the impossible? Kate squeezed her eyes tightly closed and willed herself not to think about the future, or the consequences of what they had done, just to concentrate on here and now.

She turned slightly so that she was facing him and then reached to kiss him. He smiled sleepily and she kissed him again; his arms tightened around her, drawing her naked body closer to his. Then he was kissing her back and drawing her underneath him with a sleepy low growl of seduction. And once more they were lost in each other, carried away with the desire and pleasure of the moment.

The sun stole stealthily across the luxurious bedroom, lighting up the gold covers thrown back from the bed.

Kate opened her eyes and blinked. Then looked across at the pillow next to her. Nick was fast asleep.

She remembered how he'd undressed her and carried her in here last night, how he'd tenderly, with infinite care, made love to her. The memory was so sensual that she felt herself melt inside all over again.

But where did they go from here?

The question, unbidden, ran through her mind. Suddenly she was in uncharted waters with Nick. They had always known where they stood with each other, what they could expect from each other, and now she had this stomach-churning feeling that she had blown it.

Was she destined to be like all the other women in his life, desired for a short time and then discarded when he got bored? And if and when that time came, would that be the end of their friendship?

She looked over at Nick and wanted to move into his arms again, but she knew where that would lead and she needed to think about things before they went any further. For a while she watched him as he slept. He looked different somehow, more vulnerable than the mighty, confident Nick she knew so well. She longed to kiss the sensual curve of his lips, run her fingers over the powerful breadth of his shoulders. Her eyes moved lower to where the sheet rested on the taut, flat stomach. The longing to touch him became so intense that she had to make herself move away from him.

Kate slipped gently out of the bed. Her heart was thumping against her chest as she quickly rifled through her case and took out a black pair of jogging trousers and a pink sports top. She slipped into them and then, picking up her trainers, she stole out of the room. What she needed was an early morning jog to clear her mind, and help her think about the way forward. And she knew that the hotel had extensive grounds with a jogging track that led along the side of the beach.

It was just eight o'clock as she stepped out of the main entrance of the hotel. Although the sun was up, it was a cool, misty morning, perfect for running. She followed the arrows towards the beach and set off at a brisk pace, putting her hair back in a pony-tail as she went.

Jogging was something Kate did frequently at weekends and it always made her feel better. This morning, however, peace of mind was hard to come by. She kept thinking about Nick lying in that enormous four-poster bed, and wishing she were still up there with him.

One thing was clear to her. She was definitely in love with Nick; it certainly wasn't an imaginary feeling. This was the real thing. She knew now what she'd felt for Stephen had never been anything even close to this. It was no wonder she'd had doubts when she'd thought Stephen wanted to marry her. Yes, she had cared about Stephen, had fun with him…had affection for him. But her feelings for him paled into insignificance next to the magnitude of her feelings for Nick. She knew that this was the man she wanted to spend the rest of her life with, and she knew it with a mind-blowing certainty that she had never felt with Stephen.

So what was she going to do about it? She needed to plan a way forward so that she could face him this morning with some semblance of confidence.

She knew that he wasn't into commitment, and that all the women who had got serious about him had been thrown over. So how could she make sure that she was different?

Perhaps the fact that she knew him better than anybody would work in her favour? For instance, she knew exactly his likes and his dislikes. Knew that women who threw themselves at him only lasted a short time. Knew that he panicked given a woman who crowded him. So maybe she should do the opposite. Pretend she was as cool and together as he was. Act as if last night had been wonderful, but that she didn't expect anything else. And maybe…just maybe it would work in her favour. What was it he had said about Stephen: 'He only wants you back now because he thinks he can't have you…'?

Maybe the same could be said of Nick. And if playing it cool backfired she might at least manage to salvage their friendship out of the wreckage. It was a chance worth taking.

The beach lay before her now and Kate stopped, taking deep gulps of the fresh morning air, watching the way the sun glinted on the water as it lapped against the shore. Life felt good again, full of promise.

Then she saw Stephen jogging towards her from the other direction and groaned.

She made to turn away but he had already spotted her. 'Morning, Kate,' he called cheerfully.

'Morning.'

'I was hoping I'd bump into you—it's lonely jogging on your own.' He stopped next to her and leaned his hands on his knees, wheezing.

'You're out of condition,' she remarked.

He slanted a wry look up at her. 'That's because I haven't got you to motivate me. I haven't been jogging since we split up.'

'Well, go jogging with Natasha, then,' Kate said briskly.

Stephen pulled a face. 'She's into some new-wave exercise craze. She sits cross-legged and bounces on a large rubber mat from one side of her living-room floor to the other. Can you imagine me doing that?'

Kate stared at him for a moment, and her lips twisted with amusement at the picture he'd conjured up. 'No, Stephen, I can't. But then I'm the last person to know what you're capable of.'

Stephen ignored that. 'Can I jog back to the hotel with you?' he asked hopefully.

By the look of his red face, she didn't think he'd be keeping up with her. 'If you want.' She glanced at her watch. 'We'd better get a move on, though. I'd like some breakfast before I leave today.'

Surprisingly Stephen seemed to get a second wind and he did keep up with her for a while. But his downfall was that he kept trying to have a conversation with her.

Kate really didn't want to hear about Natasha's fetish for goat's milk or the fact that her fridge was full of health food, and lengthened her stride down by the hotel gardens so that he fell behind. 'Don't forget to come and collect your stuff,' she called back to him. 'I'm going to move out of the apartment soon and, unless you take it, it'll get thrown away.'

Nick was on his mobile phone when she stepped back into their room. He was wearing a suit and he looked ready to go, his bag packed and sitting by the door.

'I'll get the champagne,' he was saying in a low voice, 'And you…' He turned at the sound of her closing the door, and smiled at her.

She felt her heart start to speed up, felt her body tighten with a warm, gloriously sensual feeling. How the hell was she ever going to manage to play this cool? she wondered wryly.

'Hi.' His eyes flicked over her slender figure, making her feel as vulnerable as if she had nothing on.

'Hi.' Kate smiled hesitantly back.

'Won't be a minute,' he said quietly before turning his attention back to the phone. 'No, don't worry about dinner,' he told whoever was on the other end. 'We'll get a take-away.'

Who was he talking to? she wondered. Whoever it was, it didn't sound like a business call.

She went quietly through to the bedroom and closed the door behind her.

The rumpled sheets on the bed and her clothing on the floor brought back vivid memories of the night before, making her heart race.

Kate headed into the bathroom, stripping off her clothes as she went. Just remember to play it cool, she told herself as she stood under the forceful jet of the shower.

She groaned and turned her face under the jet of water, as if it could wash away all the impure thoughts that plagued her. Thoughts of how handsome Nick was, how wonderful his naked body had felt against hers. She squeezed her eyes tightly closed, trying to change the line of thinking, get rid of the steamy hot images that were flicking through her head. But they refused to go.

Kate stepped out of the shower and reached blindly for a towel at the same time as the bedroom door opened and Nick came in.

She wasn't quite quick enough to cover her naked body, and as their eyes met and held through the open bathroom door there was a moment when she felt rigid with embarrassment, which was stupid because he'd seen everything there was to see last night.

Then his gaze dipped lower, and there was a gleam of male appreciation in his gaze. A look that made her body quiver as if he had physically touched her.

'You should have woken me this morning,' he said softly, sounding totally relaxed as if they spent every morning with her in a state of undress. 'I was disappointed to wake and find you gone.'

Kate wrapped the white towel firmly around her. 'Would you have come jogging with me?'

'Maybe not,' Nick murmured. The way he looked at her left her in no doubt about the direction his thoughts were taking.

She looked away from him, willing herself to stem any rising desire inside her.

He smiled. 'I'm sorry; I'm interrupting your shower. I did knock on the bedroom door.'

'I…I didn't hear you. But it's OK, I should have closed this door.'

'I'm glad you didn't.' His voice was husky.

Nick came further into the room, put his arms around her and kissed her very firmly, very possessively on the lips. She felt herself dissolve inside, all cool intentions heated to desert temperatures.

He pulled back from her and looked at her. 'We need to talk about last night,' he said gently.

'Yes…I know.'

He kissed her again, and she felt the towel slipping as he kissed her on the neck and then lower. 'Nick, we do need to talk, but…but not like this…here…' Panic-stricken, she grabbed the towel before it fell completely.

'Spoilsport.' He grinned and moved back. 'OK, you win. But only because I'm starving and would like break-fast before we leave. So don't be long.' He closed the door behind him and she sank down to sit on the side of the bath, her knees literally trembling.

'Heaven's sake, Kate,' she muttered. Get a grip. You don't want to fall to pieces around Nick. That's what women always do and it doesn't get them anywhere.

She heard the phone ring in the bedroom. It stopped

after a few rings, and she assumed Nick had picked it up in the lounge.

It was probably Reception reminding them to vacate their room by eleven, she thought, getting up to dry her hair. It didn't take long to get ready. She applied a light make-up and donned her jeans and a pale powder-blue shirt that was casual yet sexy enough to show her curves, and, with a last check to make sure she looked as good as possible, she threw her belongings in her suitcase and left the bedroom.

Nick was standing with his back to her, looking out of the window.

'Stephen has just been on the phone,' he said without turning.

'Oh? What did he want?' she asked warily.

'I don't know, he wouldn't say. Just asked if you'd phone him on his mobile.' He turned then and looked at her. 'Did you go jogging with him this morning?'

What was behind that question? Kate wondered. Was this her friend Nick, enquiring because he cared about her, or was it deeper than that?

'Not with him exactly, but...' She met his eyes and shrugged. Maybe it wouldn't do any harm to make him wonder what was going on between her and Stephen. Thinking he had a bit of competition might well make him all the keener. Might make him actively pursue her. She knew Nick loved a challenge. 'Well, yes, I suppose I did.'

'So you're friends again?'

She'd always thought she could read Nick well. There had been lots of times in the past when he'd caught her eye and she'd known exactly what he'd been thinking, probably because she'd been thinking the same thing. They'd shared many a joke like that. But now, when it really mattered, she couldn't fathom what was going on behind those dark eyes.

'I wouldn't go so far as to say we are friends,' she said. 'But I'm speaking to him. I have to, we've still got… things to work through…' She hesitated and then decided to be honest. 'But it's our friendship I'm bothered about, Nick,' she said quietly. 'I don't want to jeopardize it in any way and I'm worried that last night might.'

'We're both grown-ups, Kate,' Nick said with a shrug. 'Last night was just one of those things.'

What did he mean, 'just one of those things'? Kate frowned. She was the one supposed to be playing it cool…not him.

'Yes, I know it was.' She hoped her voice didn't sound angry; it seemed to have raised an octave.

He smiled; a lopsided smile that tugged at her emotions. 'But I did enjoy it,' he murmured huskily.

There was a knock at the door. It was the maid wanting to come in and clean the room. Lousy timing, Kate thought wryly.

'We'll talk over breakfast,' Nick said quietly. 'I'll put the cases in the car and we can leave straight after.'

Why did that sound so final? she wondered.

As Nick headed outside with the bags, Kate went down into the dining room and found a table for two next to the window. She wasn't in the slightest bit hungry now. She felt edgy, very unsure how to proceed. All her positive thoughts while she was out jogging seemed to have deserted her.

The only thing she could think was that last night was probably a terrible mistake. She really didn't want to lose Nick as a friend and that was the only way this could go.

She glanced out of the window and saw Nick walking around the side of the building; he was talking to a woman who was wearing jeans and a cropped top revealing a tanned and bejewelled belly button. She was probably about nineteen, tall and willowy, her blonde hair in plaits.

It took a few moments for Kate to recognize that it was Natasha. As soon as she did, she felt her heart nosedive somewhere down into her stomach. How dared Nick consort with the enemy? What the hell were they talking about? Natasha seemed very amused by it, whatever it was. She was looking up at him the way all women looked at him and it made Kate feel positively sick.

The waitress arrived next to the table to ask what she wanted to drink. Kate asked for a pot of tea and turned her attention back to the window. But Nick and his companion had disappeared around the side of the hotel.

Kate had ordered some toast and was on her second cup of tea by the time Nick joined her.

'What took you so long?' she asked, trying to sound nonchalant as he sat down opposite her.

'Was I long? Sorry.' Nick shrugged. 'Have you ordered?'

'Yes, I have.' She stared at him across the table. Wasn't he going to tell her that he'd been speaking to Natasha? As the silence stretched between them it seemed obvious that he wasn't…which begged the question why? She watched as he poured himself a cup of tea.

'Good view of the garden from in here.' She tried to jog him a bit.

'Yes, isn't there?' He smiled at her and stole a piece of toast from her plate. 'I think I'll have a full cooked breakfast,' he said, looking around for the waitress. 'I'm starving.'

What had happened to the days when they'd told each other everything? she wondered. It suddenly occurred to her that she didn't know Nick as well as she had thought she did.

She'd warned Jan that he was a womaniser and really she hadn't been telling lies. He did have an eye for a pretty woman.

Thinking about Jan brought a rush of colour to her cheeks and a wave of guilt. She'd forgotten all about her friend, she realized with dismay.

'Are you OK?' Nick asked her, his voice quiet, his eyes suddenly watchful.

'Yes.' She took a deep breath. 'Listen, Nick, about last night.' Her voice came out in a rush. 'I realize now that it was a mistake.'

Nick's eyes narrowed on her but he said nothing.

'I'm not thinking very clearly at the moment…my emotions are all over the place.' That at least wasn't a lie because as she met the darkness of his eyes there was part of her that was screaming, What are you saying? Don't say that. Stop it, stop it now.

'I know that, Kate.'

She was surprised by how gentle his voice was. Calm and reasoning, it brought a halt to the feverish racing of her mind.

'You haven't really had a chance to get over Stephen. It's probably too soon to dive into another relationship. I can understand that you are a bit apprehensive.'

'Can you?' Kate stared at him, her heart hammering against her chest. Was he being understanding, or did he think last night was a mistake as well?

'Yes, of course I can. We've been friends for a long time. Like you, I don't want anything to ruin that.'

She bit down on her lip. 'So what should we do—forget last night ever happened?'

'I don't think that's possible, do you?' His voice lowered huskily, sending her blood pressure soaring. 'But we'll just have to be adult about it.'

'And how do you propose we do that?' she asked.

'Remain friends.'

Kate swallowed hard. So much for playing it cool, she thought angrily. It had lasted all of an hour and then blown up in her face. 'Fine.' She looked away from him and out of the window.

Well, she'd given him a way out, and he'd taken it. Given his track record with women, maybe it was for the best.

The waitress came and took Nick's breakfast order.

'I don't know how you can eat all that,' Kate remarked as they were left alone again.

'I've worked up an appetite,' he said casually. Then watched as the colour filtered into the delicate porcelain perfection of her skin again.

She looked away from him out of the window.

Nick studied her across the breakfast table, thoughts of last night playing through his mind; the supple beauty of her body, the warmth of her kisses—the memory tore at him. He wanted to reach out and take her hand in his. In fact he wanted to say, Let's forget breakfast and ask for our room back. But he felt if he did that he might lose her altogether.

Sunlight slanted over her, highlighting the golden-red tones in Kate's glossy chestnut hair and the perfection of her skin. Her eyes were hidden from him beneath long dark lashes, but he sensed her vulnerability. Last night shouldn't have happened; he should have called a halt to it. Trouble was he had wanted her so badly. For weeks his patience and his self-control had been stretched to breaking-point. Last night he just hadn't been able to hold back any longer.

All he could do now was back off, give her space and time. He didn't want to take her back to bed if she was on the rebound. Hell, that wouldn't be good for either of them and would certainly wreck the friendship.

'What did Natasha say to you in the garden?' she asked him suddenly.

Nick frowned. He had half hoped when he'd made her blush that she might have been thinking about what had happened between them last night. Not bloody Stephen.

'Natasha?'

'Bimbo with body piercing,' Kate said succinctly.

'Actually she's a very intelligent woman, not a bimbo,' Nick said irritably.

'How would you know?' Kate frowned. 'She gave you her CV while you were putting the bags in the car, did she? No wonder you were a long time.'

'No, she didn't give me her CV,' Nick remarked lightly. 'I've met her before. She used to work at a company I contracted to for a while.'

He had never noticed just how brightly emerald-green Kate's eyes were. 'Why didn't you tell me that when you saw her yesterday?' she asked.

'I didn't recognize her yesterday.' Nick reached and poured himself another cup of tea. 'But she remembered me.'

Kate found it hard to believe that any man wouldn't remember Natasha. She was very attractive. 'So you just talked about work, then?' she probed curiously.

'Well, we didn't talk about Stephen, if that's what you're asking.'

'No, it wasn't what I was asking.'

Nick looked unconvinced.

Kate fell silent for a moment. She was stunned that Nick knew Natasha. Of course, he had always had a weakness for blondes. Did he find her very attractive? Jealousy and curiosity twisted inside her.

'According to Stephen, she's a bit of a health freak.'

'Is she?' Nick shrugged. 'She can't be that much of a health freak—it seems that she wasn't out jogging this morning.'

'No. Apparently she does some New Age bouncing in the living room.'

'That sounds interesting,' Nick murmured.

Kate fell silent. He would think that sounded interesting, she thought derisively. But she had her answer; it was obvious from that gleam in his eye that Nick could see the attraction of Natasha all too clearly.

The waitress brought Nick's breakfast and a fresh pot of tea.

'What are you doing about your apartment?' he asked, taking the opportunity to change the subject.

'Well, as I have to be out of there in four weeks I'm going to have to start flat-hunting in earnest.'

'Do you want me to give you a hand? I'll be around all next week.'

'No. I'll manage, thank you.' Her voice was stiff. She was annoyed with him, and even more annoyed with herself for giving a damn about his opinion of Natasha.

It didn't really matter whether he knew Natasha or found her attractive. The bottom line was that he regretted last night...that was the bit that really stung her already fragile confidence.

'Just ring me if you change your mind,' he said. 'I've got a good eye for property.'

It wasn't the only thing he had a good eye for, Kate thought dryly. But then she had always known that. So the fact that she was feeling like this was just her own damn fault.

CHAPTER EIGHT

'ARE you meeting Nick for coffee?' Jan asked as they were finishing work on Monday.

Kate had really hoped that the subject of Nick wouldn't come up today. She'd been avoiding Jan as much as possible and she'd intended to make her escape before the woman had time to ask her anything. But it had been an impossible idea, she realized now. Jan had no intention of letting her get away without quizzing her. 'No, I haven't got time. I've got to go and view apartments.'

'You haven't said anything about the wedding—did you have a good time?' Jan asked curiously.

'Yes, it was very nice.' Kate hoped her skin wasn't as pink as it felt. 'What about you—did you have a good weekend?' She changed the subject swiftly.

'Yes, it was good. I went to that party.'

Kate listened idly as her colleague chatted. But at the back of her mind she was thinking about Nick.

They'd hardly spoken on the way home from the wedding. And when he'd carried her bag into her apartment for her, she hadn't asked him to stay and have a drink as she normally would have. She'd felt awkward and unsure, the old easiness that had used to exist between them had completely gone and she just hadn't known how to handle it.

'I'm seeing Nick tomorrow night,' Jan said suddenly, gaining her full attention. 'Well, I'm supposed to be, but he hasn't rung me yet.'

'Did he say he'd ring you?' Kate asked.

'To be honest I can't remember how we left it. But I'll just give him a ring anyway—I've got his mobile number.'

Kate busied herself tidying the papers on her desk, rearranging the files, and tried not to think about Jan and Nick going out together. Tried even harder not to think about how she had spent Saturday night with him. Guilt and remorse shredded through her, but there was also an overwhelming feeling of longing, a feeling she tried very hard to ignore.

What had happened between her and Nick was wrong, she told herself fiercely. He was her best friend and that friendship was far too precious to risk. She didn't know what she had been thinking about on Saturday night—maybe she was on the rebound from Stephen—but, whatever the reason, she would have to stop thinking about Nick in this way.

'Hope he's not somewhere foreign,' Jan continued. 'Last time I phoned him he was in Stockholm. I thought he said he was at home and I chatted to him for quite a while before I realized my mistake.' She rolled her eyes. 'I'm dreading getting my phone bill.'

Kate grimaced in sympathy.

'He's a hard man to pin down, isn't he?' Jan said airily.

'Yes, he is.' Kate slipped a manuscript she wanted to read later into her bag. Her empathy for Jan still tinged with an awful sense of remorse. She should never have gone to that wedding. Should have followed her instincts and stayed far away. The situation she was in now was awful; she felt terrible because of Jan. She liked Jan...she'd introduced her to Nick, for heaven's sake! What the hell had she been thinking of to do that?

She tried to comfort herself with the fact that Jan had strong-armed her into it, but, even so, it was a poor consolation. If Jan knew about her and Nick on Saturday night... She'd be upset. Even if she tried to explain it was a mistake and wasn't likely to ever happen again, Jan would probably be angry. Kate didn't want to hurt anyone like that; she knew all too well just how it felt.

'You don't have Nick's home phone number, do you?' Jan asked her suddenly.

'Sorry?' Kate glanced across at her colleague blankly.

'I was just thinking, it would be better to call Nick at home than on his mobile.'

Kate hesitated for a second. If Nick hadn't given Jan his home number, did that mean he didn't want her to have it?

'Well...' Kate stammered indecisively, then glanced across at her colleague, who was watching her with huge baby blue eyes. Heaven's sake, give her the number, she told herself briskly. Nick could handle himself—he was a grown-up. Or at least that was what he'd been telling her on Sunday morning.

It was nearing ten o'clock when Kate got home, her feet were aching, she was tired and hungry, but more depressing was the fact that she hadn't seen one apartment that she liked.

She was just about to put her front-door key in the lock when she noticed that the front lounge light was on. She frowned. That was strange; she didn't think she'd left a light on this morning.

She leaned over the railing of the step and tried to peer through the window to see if she could make out anything suspicious. She couldn't really see properly; it was too awkward an angle. So she climbed over the railing and put her foot on one of the tall plant pots to balance her weight.

That was a bit better; she could see now. She pressed her nose closer to the glass and had a brief glimpse of a man carrying a tray through from the kitchen.

Kate was so surprised that she nearly lost her balance and just managed to jump to safety on the steps before the plant pots fell over with a crash.

The front door swung open and light flooded over her as Stephen came rushing out.

'Kate! What the heck are you doing?'

'Well, I'm practising to join the circus, of course,' she grated sardonically. Then glared at him. 'More to the point, what are you doing in the apartment? And how did you get in?'

'I've still got a key.' He reached to give her a hand to climb back over the other side of the wrought-iron rails. 'As you weren't here I thought I'd collect my belongings.' He didn't let go of her hands, just stood staring into her eyes. 'Hell, Kate, I miss you so much,' he said gently. 'Things with Natasha just aren't working out.'

'I'm sorry, Stephen,' Kate said, genuinely sympathetic. 'But it's none of my business now. It's over between us and we both have to get on with our lives.'

Stephen nodded, looking resigned and sad. 'I'll always care about you, Kate. And I'll always regret the mistakes I've made.'

As Nick drove around the corner he saw Kate standing on her doorstep with Stephen. They were holding hands. As he watched they turned and went into the house together, closing the front door.

There was a space further down the road and he pulled into it, and then sat drumming his fingers impatiently on the steering wheel, watching the front door in his rear-view mirror.

Stephen didn't come back out again. So much for giving Kate space and time to get over the guy, Nick thought angrily. She was obviously as besotted as ever.

For a moment he found himself thinking about their night together, the sensual curve of her body, the way she had responded to his kisses. Angry with himself, he started the car and drove away. He shouldn't have made love to her on Saturday. He had known that it was probably too soon, that she was in all probability still on the rebound. Had seriously mucked up after all his good intentions of just being there for her and helping her. Patience had never been his strong suit and, where Kate was concerned, it had been severely tested for some time.

But there was no point dwelling on what had happened between them—clearly Kate wasn't, and if he wanted to keep her friendship he'd have to respect that and move forward.

When he got into his apartment the light was flashing on his answer machine. He pressed play and listened to three messages; all were from Jan.

Nick frowned. He didn't think he'd given Jan his home phone number. Then realization dawned. Kate couldn't have made it any clearer to him if she had put up a sign in neon lights saying 'stay away'.

He sat thinking for a while, and then resolutely lifted up the phone. If that was the way Kate wanted to play it, then so be it, he thought grimly.

The office was quiet, most of the staff having gone for lunch. The silence was wonderful; even the phone hadn't rung for half an hour. Kate flicked through the manuscript before her, and read over her notes. It was pleasant working at lunch, she decided. Maybe she should do it more often. She glanced over at Jan's desk, wondering if she was working through her lunch-hour as well.

Jan was reading a magazine. Kate did a double take as she noticed it was a bridal magazine.

'Great article in here on Christmas weddings,' Jan remarked as she caught Kate's gaze. 'Very romantic.'

'Really?' Kate's voice was a strangled whisper. She glanced back at her work, her tranquillity and her concentration broken.

Was Jan getting serious about Nick? It certainly looked that way. Maybe she should tell her again that Nick wasn't into commitment. Try and warn her in case she got hurt? She glanced back at her colleague, opened her mouth, and then closed it again. It was none of her business, and, besides, maybe she'd just sound jealous.

It was nearly two weeks now since Kate had gone to Tanya's wedding and she hadn't seen Nick since. But Jan had. Jan had been out to dinner, and to the theatre, had even enjoyed an evening clubbing with him. Kate tried not to ask, tried to switch off as soon as his name was mentioned, but it was extremely hard not to be curious, not to care. Every time she heard his name she felt an ache of emptiness deep inside that was like nothing she had ever experienced before.

'How are things with you and Nick?' The question blurted out, she couldn't help it, couldn't restrain herself.

'Fine. I'm meeting him for coffee after work—why don't you come along?'

'No, thanks; I've got more flats to look at. I just wondered how he was…that's all.'

Jan looked up across the office and smiled. 'Well, speak of the devil, you can ask him yourself.'

Kate looked quickly around. Nick had just come in and

was sauntering across the large open-plan office as if he lived there.

She felt her heart miss several beats as she looked over and met his eyes. He was wearing a dark blue suit with an open-necked pale blue shirt beneath it. As always, he looked confident and extremely handsome.

'Hi, how are you doing, Kate?' He smiled as he stopped in front of her desk.

'Fine, Nick, how are you?' She cringed. They sounded like total strangers. Suddenly the memory of their night together ran vividly through her mind. The touch of his hands against her skin, the taste of his kisses, the feeling of complete and utter bliss, all of it in a fast-forward replay that brought heat and longing racing through her.

'How's the flat-hunting going?' he asked.

'I haven't found anywhere I like yet. It's proving more difficult than I thought it would be. But I'm working on it.' She smiled.

'I'm sure something will turn up.' He glanced over at Jan. 'I thought I'd take you up on that offer of coffee.'

'Coming right up.' Jan grinned. She got up from her desk and walked across to reach up and kiss him on the cheek. The easy familiarity brought a lump to Kate's throat. Not too long ago that would have been her, kissing Nick, smiling at him, completely relaxed.

'Would you like a coffee?' Jan asked her, standing with her arm linked through Nick's.

'Yes, thank you, Jan.' Kate returned her attention to her work, but it was a futile gesture, because she was very aware of Nick's every move. He went across to sit on the edge of Jan's desk as she went to get their drinks. Out of the corner of her eye she saw him lift the magazine that Jan had been reading.

What did he make of that? she wondered dryly.

'How's Stephen?' Nick asked

'Oh, he's OK.' Kate shrugged. 'Still with Natasha, I believe.'

'Really? I heard they'd split up.'

'Did you?' Kate frowned. She hadn't heard that. In fact since the night Stephen had come around to the apartment and taken away his things she hadn't heard anything from him. 'Where did you hear that?'

Nick shrugged. 'I can't remember.'

'What's that?' Jan asked as she came over with three mugs balanced precariously in her hands.

'I was just asking Kate if she'd heard that Stephen and Natasha have split up.'

Jan put Kate's coffee down beside her. 'If that's the case, maybe you two will get back together,' she said cheerfully.

'I wouldn't hold my breath on that one,' Kate said firmly.

'In that case, why don't you meet Andre?' Jan said suddenly. 'We could all go for supper tonight? What do you say, Kate?'

'I told you, I'm flat-hunting and—'

'Well, you've got to eat. We could meet up later, say nine?'

Kate glanced over at Nick; the thought of having dinner with him made her emotions churn like butter. He was watching her quietly, his eyes slightly narrowed.

She found the way he was studying her unnerving. He probably felt as uncomfortable as herself about the idea of a foursome for supper.

Jan started to flick through her address file on the computer. 'Now, I have Andre's number somewhere in here,' she said absently.

'Don't ring him, Jan!' Kate was horrified.

'Don't be such a stick-in-the-mud,' Jan answered airily. 'It's one meal, not an arranged marriage.'

Kate glanced over and met Nick's gaze again. He looked faintly amused. That really irritated her. It made her pull herself up, change tack. If he thought she was running scared, that she was too afraid to go out in a foursome with him, he could take a running jump. She wasn't afraid of anybody.

'So what's Andre really like?' she asked Jan abruptly.

'I told you, he's nice. Good-looking, charming…I think you'll like him.'

'But what about Stephen?' Nick asked quietly.

Kate shrugged. 'What about Stephen?' she said indifferently. 'He's not living with me any more. I can see who I want.'

Jan smiled. 'Hold that thought,' she said, lifting her phone and dialling.

Nick was watching her with that slightly narrow-eyed look again. She could hardly listen to Jan's conversation without wondering what was going through his mind.

'You don't really want to go out with this Andre guy, do you?' he asked suddenly, quietly.

She shrugged and wanted to say, What's it got to do with you anyway? But she refrained. 'Maybe I just need to play the field for a while,' she said instead.

'Make Stephen sweat it out a bit longer before you move him back in?'

Kate glared at Nick. 'I don't think that's any of your business,' she said sharply.

Jan put the phone down and then looked from Kate to Nick. 'Andre can't make it tonight, it will have to be tomorrow.'

'Tomorrow is fine by me,' Nick said indifferently. His

eyes met Kate's and she wondered if she was imagining the light of challenge in them.

'Yes...tomorrow is great,' she said cheerily.

Nick finished his coffee and got up from the desk. 'Well, I'll leave you two ladies to your work,' he said casually.

'I'll walk out with you,' Jan said, standing up.

'See you tomorrow, Kate,' Nick said with a wry smile as they left.

Why was Jan walking out of the building with him? Kate wondered. Was it so she could kiss him? The picture of them entwined in each other's arms in the lift made her go cold inside.

Had Nick fallen for Jan? Maybe he had. He certainly hadn't missed a beat when he'd picked up that bridal magazine. And Nick taking time off work to come in here for a coffee was a bit strange. She tried to dismiss the notion. Nick was phobic about marriage. Of course he wasn't getting serious.

But then she found herself remembering all those stories about men who'd shunned commitment for years, only to meet someone unexpectedly and get married within weeks. It did happen.

It was a while before Jan returned to her desk. 'I've just been giving Nick a guided tour of the place,' she said. 'He was very impressed.'

With what? Kate wondered. 'Things are heating up between you two, then?' she asked casually.

'Yes, but I could do with them heating up a bit more...if you get my meaning.' Jan smiled. 'Trouble is...there's someone else...someone I just can't get off my mind.'

Kate nearly knocked her coffee over in surprise. 'I thought you really liked Nick?'

'I do.' Jan picked up her wedding magazine again. 'He's exciting and great fun to be with, and sometimes when I look at him I feel my stomach flip... Do you know what I mean?'

'Yes. I know exactly what you mean,' Kate said quietly.

'But he's a free spirit, isn't he? One week he's in Stockholm, the next London. And women throw themselves at him. I just know that Nick is not the settling-down type. And it's made me think again about...this other man.'

Kate felt herself heave a sigh of relief. She was right. Nick wasn't the settling-down type. 'So who is this other guy?' she asked curiously.

'You don't know him,' Jan said quickly.

'So, are you two-timing Nick?' Kate was astounded.

'Not two-timing exactly,' Jan said cautiously. 'I mean, it's early days yet. I'm just rethinking things.'

Kate didn't get a chance to follow this up because her phone started ringing and people started to filter back into the office as the day's work suddenly thrust in on them again.

Looking around flats alone was depressing, Kate decided as she let herself into her apartment later that evening. Or maybe it was just the fact that everything she liked was out of her price league.

She went through to the lounge, flicking on the lights. There were two messages on her answer machine. She flicked them on. The first was from her mother. 'Just ringing to see how you are,' she said cheerily.

The second was from Tanya. 'Just back from honeymoon,' she said hurriedly. 'We've had a fabulous time. But really I was just ringing to see if you'd heard the news? Apparently Stephen and Natasha are engaged! Ring me when you have a minute.'

Kate frowned. That couldn't be right…surely? Stephen hadn't seemed happy last time she'd seen him. And Nick had said he thought they had split up!

She was about to replay the message, thinking maybe she'd misheard, then changed her mind and pressed erase. She didn't have the energy to listen to that again. Stephen was out of her life and how he chose to vacillate in his private life was nothing to do with her any more.

Bath and bed were all she really wanted; however, she supposed she had better eat something. She opened and closed kitchen cupboards, but there was nothing remotely tempting to be found in them. If this continued she'd be like a stick insect; she'd already lost half a stone since Stephen had left.

Maybe the up side of all this was that now she had a very flat stomach she could have her belly button pierced, she thought wryly. That would shake Nick tomorrow, if she arrived to supper in a figure-hugging outfit with a diamond in her navel. She grinned at the picture she conjured up in her mind of Nick's startled face.

She realized that she was standing staring into the fridge and had completely forgotten what she was doing. Hell, she had it bad, she thought as she slammed the door closed again. She couldn't get Nick out of her mind. More than anything else she missed him. Missed not being able to lift the phone and speak to him when she felt like it…go around when the mood struck… What was she going to do?

Just don't think about him, she told herself sternly. She went through to the lounge and lifted the morning paper. Sit and unwind and don't think about anything. She flicked over the pages to see if she could find any good news. She found the horoscopes.

According to the blurb, Nick was having a difficult time, an affair was going badly wrong and for once the resolute Gemini was undecided about how to proceed.

That should have cheered Kate up. But surprisingly it didn't. If Nick was upset about Jan then he must be smitten. What was Jan's star sign?

The doorbell rang, interrupting the silence of the apartment and her active imagination.

A dart of surprise and pleasure shot through her as she drew back the bolts and opened the door to find Nick standing on her doorstep.

'Hi.' Kate stared at him, her heart thundering at about a million miles an hour. He was wearing jeans and a pale grey shirt. He looked great. She would have liked to go into his arms saying, Thank heavens you're here, I miss you. Instead she said coolly, 'What are you doing here?'

One eyebrow lifted wryly. 'Do I have to have an excuse to visit you now?'

Her heart melted in an instant. 'No, of course not.' She stepped back and opened the door wider. 'What I meant was, I thought you would be out with Jan tonight.'

'She's busy, catching up with something around the house.'

Her mystery man, probably, Kate thought, not knowing whether to feel sympathy for Nick or annoyance that the only reason he had come around here was because he was at a loose end.

'Would you like a drink?' she asked as he followed her into the lounge.

'I'll have a cup of tea. Thanks.'

He sat down in the lounge as she went to put the kettle

on. When she returned with the drinks, he was reading the paper that she had left open.

'I see that you've been researching your future,' he observed dryly. 'Apparently Sagittarians are moving into a very positive and romantic phase of their lives.'

'Really.' Kate put the tray down on the table.

'And there's a full moon in a critical point in your chart.' He glanced over at her. 'Does that mean Stephen will be howling outside your door tonight?'

'It means I'm in no mood for your dry humour, Nick,' she said, handing him the cup of tea.

Nick's eyes drifted over her slender figure. She was wearing a pair of black trousers and a yellow top. She looked attractive...possibly too attractive for his peace of mind. 'What's the problem? Things not going to plan between you and Stephen?'

She swung her head around to look at him, her hair swishing silkily back from her face in a straight glossy curtain. 'There is no plan between Stephen and me.'

'What star sign is he?' Nick asked, glancing back at the paper. 'Maybe it will tell you what to do in here.'

'He's an Aries. Now, will you cut it out, Nick?'

'Maybe you should cut it out,' he muttered, reading the horoscope and deliberately misinterpreting her words. 'It says here that he's unstable and in a state of flux.'

'You're just making that up,' Kate said crossly.

Nick ignored her. 'You know, this stuff isn't bad. Maybe I should start reading it on a regular basis.'

She wanted to ask if he was as troubled in his relationship with Jan as it said, but to ask would be to admit she had already read his horoscope and she wasn't going to give him that satisfaction. He was big-headed enough.

'Does it say in there where I might be moving to?' she

asked instead, her voice as sarcastic as his. 'I could do with a bit of help on the home front.'

He glanced up at her and grinned. 'Hey, it's my job to mock the horoscopes…not yours. You're not turning into a cynic, are you?'

'No. I'm just turning into a very tired person who hasn't eaten.'

Nick looked thoughtful for a moment. 'I haven't eaten either. How about going for a pizza with me?' he said. 'I know a really nice Italian restaurant.'

She settled herself in the chair opposite and tucked her feet up underneath her, like a cat curling up by the fire. 'Another time, maybe, Nick,' she murmured.

Nick watched her, noted the way she didn't quite meet his eye as she turned him down.

He looked back at the paper. 'Hold on a minute, it says in here, Sagittarians must not, on their peril, turn down an offer from a tall handsome man, for fear of starvation setting in.'

'Does it say when this tall handsome man might be arriving?' Kate asked, slanting a teasing glance over at him.

Nick grinned, and for a moment as their eyes met that old easy relationship was there again between them, strong and reassuring.

He put the paper down. 'So what do you say? Shall we go and grab something to eat together?'

Kate hesitated. 'I don't think it's a good idea, Nick,' she said, trying to be level-headed.

'Why not?'

'Well…' She shrugged uneasily. 'What would Jan say?'

'What's it got to do with Jan?' Nick asked irately. 'Anyway, I'm suggesting we eat food, not each other.'

He watched as her cheeks flared with colour. 'Jan's busy doing something else. I'm hungry, so are you.' He met her eyes directly. 'What's the problem?'

She knew what he was saying to her. She'd had drinks and meals with him in the past when he'd been dating other women and neither of them had ever thought twice about it. It was just two friends sharing some time together. But now…now it felt different.

'So shall we go?' Nick finished his tea and got to his feet. He came over and took her drink from her to put it down on the table. 'Come on, I'll buy dinner and you can tell me all about the flats you've viewed.' He held his hand out to her.

She looked up into the darkness of his eyes and then put her hand into his, allowing him to help her to her feet.

'Bang goes my diet,' she said dryly, trying to cover the wild exhilaration that raced through her the moment their skin touched.

He smiled. 'When have you ever needed to diet?' he asked softly.

For a fraction of a second they stared into each other's eyes. Kate wanted to go into his arms; the desire was intense. She didn't know if she was relieved or disappointed when he turned away and picked up his car keys from the table.

'I won't be a minute. I'll just freshen up.' She headed down to her bedroom. It was strange—she had felt tired before, and if someone had told her she'd have to go out again tonight she would have groaned and said no way, but now she felt revitalized. Filled with enthusiasm and excitement. She flicked a brush through her hair and wondered if she should get changed.

While Nick waited impatiently for her in the hall, his eyes were drawn to the cupboard where he had put the bag containing some of Stephen's belongings a few weeks ago. On impulse he opened the door and looked inside.

Stephen's bag still sat there, staring at him mockingly. He closed the door again quickly, irritated with himself for looking.

'OK, I'm ready.' Kate appeared out of her bedroom. She had changed into a blue dress; it was casual yet on her looked sensational.

He wondered how she would react if he told her that the thought of her had constantly plagued his senses. In fact since their night together he just hadn't been able to get her out of his head.

'You didn't need to get changed,' he said, almost wishing she hadn't. Maybe the trousers and top would have been less of a distraction, less of a temptation.

She was disconcerted by the disapproval in his tone. 'Don't you like this dress?' she asked, glancing at herself in the hall mirror.

'It's fine…'

She looked over at him and he smiled. 'Actually, it's more than fine,' he murmured huskily, making her blood flow as if it were on fire through her veins. 'Now, come on, let's go.'

She followed him outside and across the road to his car. This is just supper with an old friend, Kate told herself briskly. But no matter how many times she said the words, it still felt as if she was lying to herself.

CHAPTER NINE

A COOL breeze whipped in from the canal. Summer seemed to be on its way out, Kate thought as she pulled on her cardigan and then settled herself in the comfortable sports car.

As the powerful engine flared to life and they made their way across town, Nick tried not to notice the tantalizing aroma of her perfume. His eyes flicked to the long length of her legs and then quickly back to the road.

'How's work?' she asked, casting about in her mind for the topics they usually discussed.

'Same as ever.' His eyes flicked again to her legs, noting how her skirt had ridden up as she'd crossed them.

It was starting to go dark, a splattering of rain fell and Nick turned on the windscreen wipers, and for a while their gentle swish was the only sound between them.

Kate glanced at his hands on the steering wheel and suddenly she was thinking about the night they had spent together, the pleasure of being in his arms.

She turned her eyes resolutely back to the road in front. 'Have you been away on business lately?' she asked.

'A brief trip to Stockholm.'

She waited for him to elaborate but he didn't. 'You're not in a very talkative mood tonight, are you, Nick?'

'Depends what you want to talk about,' he said as he pulled the car into a space overlooking one of the canals. He looked over at her then, and the gleam in his eye was slightly disquieting.

What did he mean by that? Kate wondered nervously.

She hoped he didn't want to discuss what had happened between them at the wedding. She still hadn't really got her head around that; she certainly didn't feel confident enough to be able to casually talk about it now.

If he apologized she'd be humiliated; if he said, You were right, it was a mistake, I'm glad we can forget about it, carry on as usual, she'd be upset. It was best not to touch the subject at all.

She looked away from him and peered out of the car. It had stopped raining now and she noticed they were in one of the most fashionable areas of town.

'Come on, we'll go and eat,' Nick said, reaching for the door handle.

She followed him out of the car and they crossed the quiet street towards a brightly lit bistro with a red-and-white-striped awning.

'I had a meal in here last week and it was very enjoyable,' Nick said as he opened the door for her.

Was this where he had brought Jan? she wondered.

A waiter seated them at a table for two in the corner. It was a romantic restaurant, candlelight flickering on every table, a place for couples to sit quietly gazing into each other's eyes.

Nick ordered a bottle of wine as they perused the menu.

'I haven't eaten yet because I've been so busy looking at flats—what's your excuse?' Kate asked.

'I've been pretty busy,' he replied, pouring out the wine.

Not too busy to come and see Jan in the office today, she thought, but refrained from making the remark.

The waiter returned and took their order. Kate decided on pasta while Nick requested a steak and salad.

When they were left alone again, Kate decided to be

courageous and asked the question that was burning inside.

'How are things between you and Jan?'

Nick took a drink of his wine. 'Not bad.'

'Not bad?' She smiled at his cool nonchalance. 'Are you talking about the alcohol or the woman?'

'The woman, of course.' He grinned teasingly. 'The wine is exceptional.'

'Nick!' She gave him a reproachful look; Jan was her friend, after all.

He held up his hands. 'Only joking.'

There was silence again between them. Was he joking, or not? It was hard to tell. Nick had always been the perfect gentleman where his girlfriends were concerned. Even when they'd really irritated him, or things weren't so good in a relationship, he usually refrained from talking about it, or made light of it.

Kate darted a hesitant glance across at him. 'I figured you must be kind of smitten as you haven't been over to see me in a while.'

'That works both ways,' Nick said seriously. 'You haven't been round to my place in a while.'

'Well, you know how it is...' She shrugged. 'I've been really busy looking around flats.'

His gaze moved over her, and for a moment lingered on her lips.

The look made Kate tremble inside. It also stirred up a storm of longing.

'So, apart from having difficulty finding a new flat, everything is OK with you?' he asked quietly.

'Yes, of course.' Was her voice too bright? she wondered.

'And we're still friends?'

The question caused a ripple of disquiet inside her. 'Of course we are. Why would you think otherwise?'

One eyebrow rose and he met her eyes with a hint of sarcasm. 'Just thought I'd ask,' he said dryly.

Kate schooled her features not to show any hint of the chaos inside, She knew damn well he had been referring to their night together, but she was determined not to let him know how easily he could make mincemeat of her emotions. She had her pride, after all.

She was quite thankful that their meals arrived at that point.

'By the way, you haven't forgotten about my parents' ruby anniversary party, have you?' Nick asked once they were left alone again.

'No…' The change of conversation was welcome, but she felt wary.

'I meant to talk to you about it in the office today, and it completely slipped my mind. I'm going to book my flight and I wondered if I should book you on it as well?'

'When exactly is it?' She stalled for time, trying to gather her senses.

'The fifteenth of next month, a Saturday as luck would have it.'

Kate wanted very much to go to the party but she didn't think it was a good idea to travel with Nick—not after their last weekend together.

'Is Jan going?' she asked.

'No. It's just family.'

At one time she would have been flattered by that remark, and she supposed she still was, but there was a part of her—a part she didn't really want to acknowledge—that now felt upset by it. She was torn in two between wanting to belong as part of his family, and yet wanting something deeper from Nick. Little-sister status definitely didn't fit her any more, she realized sharply. It was like a dress that she had outgrown and, no matter how much she told herself she wanted to fit back into it, deep down she knew it was now impossible.

'I'd love to come to your parents' party,' she told him carefully. 'But I think it would be best if you go ahead and book your flight and I'll make my own travel arrangements.'

'What's the point in that?' Nick sounded impatient. 'We may as well travel together. Also I thought we could book into the hotel where the party will be held. That way we can relax and have a drink.'

Was he completely crazy? Alarm bells rang at that suggestion. She couldn't possibly stay at the same hotel as him. Not after last time. 'You just go ahead without me. I might have to work on Saturday morning anyway.' Kate took a deep breath and met his gaze. 'I'll have to check my diary.'

Or check with Stephen? Nick wondered angrily.

Hell, but she was very infuriating sometimes, he thought. She had to be the most elusive…the most stubborn…the most maddeningly gorgeous woman he had ever met.

'We'll talk about it when you've checked your diary, then,' he said, telling himself not to push her too hard. 'So tell me about the flat-hunting.' He moved the conversation along swiftly. 'Where exactly have you looked?'

She told him about the ones she had seen today after work, all a disaster. It was strange but she'd felt quite depressed when she'd looked around them, but now with Nick she found herself laughing.

'Honestly, it had no kitchen whatsoever,' she said, furnishing him with a description of the last property she had seen. 'It had all been ripped out and converted into an art studio, where the owner had a kiln to make pottery.'

'So he's got loads of dishes but no food?' Nick laughed.

'Exactly. Anyway, when I told him I really couldn't live without a kitchen, he just looked at me as if I was crazy and said there was a perfectly good Chinese across the road.'

'Now, come on, Katy, that has to be the place for you,' Nick cut in with a grin. 'Think of all those fortune cookies so near at hand!'

Kate laughed. 'You're right, I should ring him tomorrow and tell him I've changed my mind.'

'You see, a little positive thinking and everything is all right,' he said with a shrug.

Everything was all right when she was with him, Kate thought suddenly, meeting his eyes across the table.

He smiled at her and she felt a rush of adrenalin through her body strong enough to melt the polar ice-caps.

'Have you looked around this area?' Nick asked.

She shook her head.

'I've seen something that might interest you,' Nick said casually. 'I'll drive past it on the way home.'

Out of the corner of her eye, Kate could see the waiter hovering, waiting to see if they wanted anything else.

'Would you like a coffee, or do you want to go?' Nick asked.

She didn't want to go at all, didn't want reality to encroach upon them, but it was getting late. 'I suppose we should leave now.'

Nick summoned the waiter and paid the bill.

It was starting to rain again when they stepped outside. They stood under the awning, and he placed a detaining hand on her arm. 'You wait here, I'll get the car.'

'I'll be OK walking,' Kate said. 'It's only drizzling, I won't melt.'

Nick looked as if he was about to argue with her, but she set off at a brisk pace. The car wasn't far away, but before they were halfway across the road the rain increased, coming down in a sudden icy whoosh.

'You should have listened to me and waited,' Nick said, catching hold of her hand as they ran the last few metres laughing breathlessly.

Kate was glad that she hadn't listened. She felt alive racing through the night, the coolness of the rain against her skin, the warmth of Nick's hand in hers.

She stumbled a little as she reached the car and he put his arm around her, pulling her close in against him. She could feel the heat of his body and the longing it conjured up inside her was so sharp it was painful.

He opened the passenger door for her and she slid in.

'Are you OK?' he asked, once he'd got in behind the driving wheel.

She nodded, but she was shivering violently.

'You're freezing.' He reached into the back and brought out his jacket. 'Here. Put this around your shoulders,' he said, handing it to her and then turning on the engine so that he could get some hot air in the car.

'Better?' he asked after a while.

She nodded, feeling a total fraud. She wasn't really cold; the shivering had started as soon as he'd touched her, the desire so intense, she found it shocking.

Nick reversed the car out of the space and drove slowly down the road. Then stopped outside a very impressive townhouse.

'That's the property I was telling you about,' he said casually.

'Is it a ground-floor flat?' Kate asked hopefully. Trying to tune her mind to practicalities.

'No, it's a house, and it's for sale.'

'I think it would be a bit big for me and too pricey.'

'Would you like a nosy around anyway?' He reached into the dashboard and pulled out a set of keys. 'It's empty,' he said as he met the look of surprise in her eyes. 'It belongs to a friend of mine, and I told him I might know someone who'd be interested.'

'I'm interested,' Kate murmured. 'But I don't think it would be practical.'

'Well, the rain is stopping now—let's go and mooch around it anyway. I'd like another look at it myself.' Nick pulled into a parking space.

Kate left Nick's jacket in the car and they got out. This turn of events had startled her somewhat. When Nick had said he'd seen something she might be interested in, she hadn't thought in a million years he'd take her around it tonight!

But that was Nick all over, she thought wryly, following him through the front door of the house. He was nothing if not unpredictable.

'So who exactly owns this place?' she asked as she stood in the pitch-blackness of the hall while Nick searched along the wall for the light switch.

Kate took a step forward, stumbled over something and nearly fell.

Lights flicked on, and Kate found herself standing in a very elegant entrance with a grand curving staircase.

Kate leaned against the antique armchair she had so nearly fallen over. 'Wow!' she said, looking around in total awe. 'What a fantastic house.'

'Thought you'd like it.' Nick glanced over at her. She was rubbing her foot.

'Did you hurt yourself?'

'No, just banged my ankle.' She looked around. 'Nick, this place is beautiful.'

Kate went over and opened a door through to the lounge. It was enormous, and beautifully furnished in the traditional period.

'I love it,' she murmured as she followed him from room to room, each one more sensational than the one before.

Upstairs, there were three bedrooms and two bathrooms.

Nick opened the door through to the master bedroom, complete with a four-poster bed. That bed reminded Kate of the one they had shared. She found herself looking at it and thinking about the way Nick had made love to her, the expert way his hands had caressed her, arousing her to fever point, her hands reaching upwards, holding the posts of the bed as she'd shuddered and moaned in complete ecstasy.

'Katy, you're so beautiful,' Nick had moaned, tasting her skin, finding her lips and hungrily devouring them as his hands had stroked over her naked body.

'So what do you think?' Nick's casual voice brought her back to the present with a sharp jolt.

'I think...' she wrenched her eyes away from the bed and then firmly reached to close the door '...that it's a family home. Totally out of my league.' She turned away from him and started to head for the staircase. 'What I need is a one-bedroomed flat. Preferably on the ground floor because I like to have a little garden to sit in—'

'This has got a pretty enclosed garden at the back, walled and fairly private,' Nick said, following her at a more leisurely pace. 'Do you want to have a look? I think there's outdoor lights—'

'There's no point, Nick.' Kate took a deep breath. 'Maybe at one time, when I was considering marriage, this would have been my dream house… It's not now. But thanks for showing me around. It was certainly interesting.'

She opened the front door. Rain was bouncing off the pavements again.

'Stay here and I'll unlock the car,' Nick said as he switched off all the lights. 'Just shut the front door behind you.'

She didn't argue.

As they drove back across town Kate's words replayed through Nick's mind. 'Maybe at one time, when I was considering marriage, this would have been my dream house… It's not now.'

Couldn't she just forget about bloody Stephen? he thought angrily. He glanced over at her; she was very quiet now, her face shuttered.

'What are you thinking about?' he asked her abruptly.

'I was wondering why you showed me that house,' she said. 'I've got a great job, but I could never afford a property like that on my own.'

'But you liked it?' Nick asked.

'There would have to be something wrong with me not to like it, but—'

'The thing is, I was thinking of buying it myself,' he interrupted her bluntly. 'I thought it might be a good investment. It's going for a very fair price.'

'Oh! I see.' Stunned, she turned in her seat to look at him. 'Are you thinking of renting it out, or converting it into apartments? That kind of thing?'

'It crossed my mind,' Nick said nonchalantly. 'I'll have to think further about it, look at the market in a bit more detail.'

The thought of that beautiful family home being turned into apartments made Kate wince. But business-wise she supposed it would make perfect sense. 'Well, you'll have to put my name down for the ground-floor apartment,' she said.

'As long as you don't want to move Stephen back in, you've got a deal,' Nick said wryly.

'I don't think a landlord has the right to be so selective,' Kate muttered. 'However, there's not much chance of that.'

He turned the windscreen wipers on as it started to rain again. 'Have you seen him at all?'

'No.'

'Not since the wedding?' he probed further.

'Oh, yes, I've seen him since then. He came around and collected his stuff.'

Nick thought about the bag full of Stephen's belongings still sitting in the hall cupboard and his hands tightened on the wheel. 'Really.' The word was filled with derisive disbelief.

'Yes, really.' She slanted a look of annoyance at him. 'And while we are on the subject of Stephen, have you really heard that he and Natasha have split up?' she asked, remembering what he'd told her in the office today and thinking suddenly about Tanya's message.

'It's not the kind of thing I'd make up, Kate,' he said. 'But I thought you said you didn't care.'

'I don't.'

'If you say so...' he drawled, his voice cool.

She frowned. 'I'm telling you the truth!'

Something about the way she looked at him made his patience snap. 'Oh, come on, Kate, who are you kidding? It's obviously a matter of time before Stephen and you are back under the same roof. All you are doing now is playing games.'

'Just because you've known me for years, Nick, don't presume you know all there is to know, because you don't,' she said tightly, annoyed by such arrogant assumptions. 'I'm not playing games; I'm playing the field. Why else do you think I've agreed to go out with Andre tomorrow night?'

He had half presumed that she was going out with Andre to make Stephen jealous. But maybe he was mistaken.

He pulled the car up outside her apartment.

'Anyway,' she said quietly, 'I heard that Stephen and Natasha were getting engaged.'

'What?' He looked at her in total amazement.

'Tanya told me.' Kate shrugged. 'But she might have got it wrong.'

All of a sudden he understood why she had sounded so upset looking around that house...a family house. 'Hell, Kate, I'm sorry. I really didn't know.'

'It's OK,' she murmured lightly.

Then as Nick continued to watch her as if she might burst into tears at any moment, she frowned. 'I'm not in love with Stephen any more, you know.' She said the words fiercely, her head held at a determined angle, her eyes glittering green-gold in the streetlight.

For a moment she reminded him of the Kate he had known as a child. He remembered how he had found her crying in the kitchen a few weeks after her father had left home. 'I don't love him anyway,' she had declared fiercely to Nick when he had tried to cheer her up.

But of course she had, she had loved him with all her heart, it had just been her way of dealing with the pain.

He wanted to put his arms around her now and tell her

everything would be all right. But he didn't dare. He knew that if he held her, he'd want more... And that wasn't fair on either of them.

'You'll get over Stephen,' he said gently instead. 'It will just take time.'

Kate glared at him, and then reached for the door handle. What was the point in talking? Nick only heard what he wanted to hear anyway.

'I'll see you tomorrow night, Nick. Thanks for dinner.'

CHAPTER TEN

KATE had been through her wardrobe several times but she still didn't know what to wear tonight. What did one wear on a blind date when the love of your life was going to be there with another woman?

She should never have agreed to this evening, she thought, feeling completely panic-stricken as she glanced at the clock. It was only the memory of Nick's patronizing speculation that she was playing games and was really still in love with Stephen that had stopped her from cancelling. She wanted to show him that he didn't know her as well as he thought he did. In fact, there was a part of her that wanted to shock him, do something outrageous...just to startle him. She wanted to prove to him that she wasn't the 'little sister', the girl who had been a part of the furniture in his life. She was a woman, a woman that men—other than Stephen—desired.

Now, with nerves spiralling, she wished she hadn't risen to this particular challenge. Just say Andre was awful? Or just say he didn't find her attractive? And meanwhile she'd have to sit watching Jan and Nick making eyes at each other.

'Big mistake, Katy,' she muttered to herself, raking through the wardrobe with the desperation of a drowning woman looking for a lifejacket. She only had half an hour to get herself together and then the taxi would be arriving.

In the end she chose a little black 'go anywhere' dress. It was hardly the most exciting of outfits, but it did flatter her slender figure and it plunged enough at the front to be provocative without being risqué.

Once she was dressed she surveyed her reflection in the mirror. She looked too pale, she needed more make-up, so she applied a brighter lipstick and consequently had to darken her eyes to balance the look.

It would have to do, she thought, picking up her beaded bag and checking that she had enough money. She intended to pay her way tonight; she didn't want to be under any obligation to Andre…to anybody.

They had arranged to meet in a bar next door to the designated restaurant because Kate hadn't wanted Andre to pick her up. She wanted to arrive and leave under her own steam—that way she could make her excuses early and escape without feeling stuck.

Exactly on time the taxi she had ordered drew up outside, and, picking up her bag and her wrap, Kate hurried out to it.

Night was falling; she watched the lights on the bridges flick on as the taxi drove her across town. For some reason, even though she was meeting up with friends, she felt lonely. Maybe it was just nerves, she thought calmly. Putting the weekend she had spent with Nick to one side, this was her first date with a man other than Stephen in nearly two and a half years.

The taxi drew up outside the bar and she got out. There was a touch of autumn in the air, she noticed, glad of the wrap around her shoulders. Leaves were falling from the trees; they crackled underfoot as she walked the few metres to the bar.

A group of people went into the bar ahead of her; they were laughing and joking and Kate suddenly felt very conscious of being on her own.

Maybe she should have agreed to going to Jan's apart-

ment and then travelled into town with her, but it was too
late for regrets.

Her head held high, she walked with far more confidence than she was feeling into the bar. It was a stylish
place, wooden polished floors and subdued lighting highlighting large vases of fragrant flowers on a long central
wooden bar. Secluded booths were strategically placed
around the perimeter and they all seemed to be filled with
laughing, gregarious people. Kate peered into the shadows, searching for a familiar face.

Then she saw Nick standing at the bar and her heart
seemed to stand still as he turned and smiled at her.

'Hi.' She needed every ounce of self-confidence to
walk towards him with a smile.

'Hi. You look good.' His eyes moved slowly over her
figure, as if committing everything about her to memory.
The look brought a fierce heat rushing through her where
there had been freezing cold moments before.

'Thank you.' He looked more than good. He was wearing a very stylish suit, probably Italian, with a designer
look about it. 'Where's Jan...?' She forced herself to
think sensibly.

'Andre said he'd pick her up. Apparently he has to pass
by her house on the way here. They'll arrive in a minute,
I'm sure.' Nick turned as the bartender came across to
them. 'What would you like to drink, Kate?'

'A glass of white wine would be nice, thank you.'

She watched as he got the drinks in. 'I'll get the next
round,' she said as he handed her the glass.

His eyebrows rose slightly, mockingly. 'You're not going to start that "I like to pay my own way" bit, are you?
You know how it irritates me when we fight over the bill.'

'I'd rather, Nick,' she said firmly. 'Besides, you bought

dinner last night—and I'm not just here with you, am I?' she reminded him.

Nick frowned. He wished she were just here with him; she looked stunningly beautiful. Andre was bound to fall head over heels. The notion inflamed his senses, tormenting him unmercifully. He didn't want to think about Kate being with another man. To counteract it, and put it in perspective, he said cheerfully, 'Well, it will just be a bit of fun tonight. I'm sure Andre will be a nice guy.'

He noticed the flicker of uncertainty in her gaze as she met his eyes. She looked nervous.

'Are you OK?' he asked softly.

'Yes, of course.'

'Hey.' He took hold of her arm and turned her to look at him. 'This is me you're talking to. Are you OK?'

'I'm fine…just a bit apprehensive.' Kate shrugged her slender shoulders. 'I was just thinking on the way here, this is the first date I've been on in years, since before Stephen. It's a bit daunting.' As she met his eyes she knew she was not only lying to him, she was lying to herself. She couldn't care less what Andre was like, or what he thought of her. It was Nick who was creating this shivery nervous apprehension in her. She was crazy about him and just seeing him like this was like a form of torture. Being with him and not being able to touch him, knowing that he was Jan's date, was like some kind of punishment.

'Well, if Andre is any kind of a man, he'll fall under your spell immediately,' Nick said gently. He reached out and touched the side of her face, his fingers sliding upwards through her hair in a swift, yet somehow provocative caress that made her senses respond wildly.

Kate looked away from him quickly in case he could see how he was affecting her. 'I don't want him to fall under my spell,' she said tentatively. 'Just a pleasant evening in relaxing company will be enough.'

'An exercise in rebuilding your confidence?'

'In a way, I suppose so.' She took another sip of her wine, trying to pull her scattered wits together. Where was the person who was going to show Nick that she was a woman who knew how to have fun, a woman used to being desired by men?

'It must have been a shock to hear that Stephen was getting engaged?' he asked suddenly, quietly, his eyes suddenly narrowed on her.

'I was surprised, certainly…but, even if it's true, I'd be stunned if Stephen actually makes it up the aisle.'

'So would I,' Nick agreed wryly.

'However, it's nothing to do with me now.' Kate took a deep breath. 'You know, Nick, this may come as a surprise to you, but my life isn't revolving around Stephen any more. I'm my own person. I'm getting on with my life and that means starting to date again…and, yes, rebuilding my confidence. And, actually, I've had quite a number of flattering offers these last few weeks. I'm starting to enjoy myself.' Liar, liar—the words shrieked in her mind, but she held her poise and his gaze. There was no point in coming tonight and playing at being a wallflower. She had a point to make and, hell, she intended to make it. 'In fact,' she continued, starting to warm to her subject, 'I'm starting to think you've had the right idea all along. Being single is enjoyable.'

'Really.' Nick's voice was quiet. 'How paradoxical, because I've just come around to your way of thinking.'

Startled, Kate looked up at him. 'My way of thinking…?'

He nodded. 'I've been giving it serious thought recently and I've decided that you were right. It's time I started to consider settling down…starting a family. In fact, playing the field is starting to bore me.' His eyes moved over her slowly, thoughtfully. 'What I need is one woman…the right woman.'

Kate had never thought she'd hear him say something like that. Shock raced through her in waves. How typical, she thought dazedly. She had set out to show him that he didn't know her as well as he thought he did, and he'd turned the tables on her.

'So what do you think?' he asked gently.

She swallowed hard. 'Well…I wish you well, of course.'

For a moment she was reminded forcibly of that afternoon months ago when she had told him that Stephen might propose to her. She remembered how she had held her breath waiting for his reaction. Of course she had been in love with him, not Stephen; she realized that now. Had hoped deep down that he would reach and take her hand and tell her that he loved her, that he wanted to settle down and she was the love of his life.

Her lips twisted wryly. That moment had really been the moment of awakening for her—not Stephen walking out. How had she been so blind? And now, when it was far too late, how could fate be so cruel that it could laugh at her like this?

She didn't have time to say anything else because at that moment they were joined by Jan and Andre.

'Hi, darling.' Jan stood on tiptoe and kissed Nick on the cheek.

Kate felt jealousy twist inside her. She remembered her conversation with Jan in the office the other day. Obviously Jan didn't realize that she had hooked Nick…that she was the woman he had chosen. Maybe the decision suddenly to play it cool and think about another man had proved the turning point, had worked for her where it had failed for Kate.

But then if someone didn't love you, all the games in the world weren't going to help, she realized bleakly.

'Hi, Kate.' Jan turned with a smile. She looked radiant in a pale yellow dress that fitted her curvaceous figure, showing it to exquisite perfection.

Would she accept Nick's proposal? Kate wondered. Then shook herself mentally. Of course she would. The only reason she had been thinking of giving Nick up was the fact that she didn't think he'd commit to her.

'Let me introduce you to Andre. Andre, this is my friend Kate and this is Nick.'

Kate snapped out of her rumination with a jolt. She had totally forgotten about Andre. She tried to look interested, and politely said hello to the man who stepped forward to shake her hand.

Jan was right; Andre was good-looking. He was about her age, blond and tall with a friendly grin. In ordinary circumstances—if her heart didn't feel as if someone had suddenly attached lead weights to it—she would have grinned back and looked forward to having a laugh this evening. As it was a smile was about as much as she could manage.

A booth nearby suddenly became vacant and Jan and Kate moved to sit down while the men got some drinks at the bar.

'Well, what do you think of Andre?' Jan asked immediately they were alone.

'He seems very nice,' Kate began cautiously.

'I think he's really handsome,' Jan said firmly. 'And he's a very successful, talented designer. I've known him for a while now. He's Dutch, born and bred here—'

Jan stopped in mid gush as the men came back. Andre sat next to Kate, Nick opposite, beside Jan.

For a while the conversation was general: the weather, TV programmes, the football season that apparently had started again. Kate listened to Jan and Andre enthuse about a match that had been played at the weekend, and frowned; she hadn't known that Jan was into football.

Across the table she met Nick's eyes and quickly she looked away again.

'So, Kate, Jan has told me that you work with her in the office?' Andre suddenly turned his attention to her.

'Yes, that's right. And I believe you are a designer?' She forced herself to move a little closer to him so that she could hear over the babble of conversation that surrounded them.

'Yes, I design gardens. I've written a few books on the subject as well. That's how I met Jan; she was my editor on one of them when she worked at another publishing house here in Amsterdam.'

'Really?' Kate found herself interested. 'I like to garden myself. I've only got a small backyard but I've put a lot of effort into creating a Mediterranean look…helped by various trips down to the flower market.'

For a while they chatted about the various types of plants and how they survived in different conditions. He really was a pleasant guy, Kate thought, warming to him.

'Shall we go to the restaurant now?' Jan interrupted abruptly when Andre stopped to gather breath.

'Yes, of course.' Andre stood up and politely helped Kate to her feet. As they left the bar, Jan fell into step next to Andre. She was asking him about work, listening with great interest to his replies. Kate slanted a glance sideways at Nick. He smiled at her. 'So far, so good…eh?'

She forced herself to smile back at him. If Nick was going to marry Jan, she was going to have to get used to nights like this. 'Yes, tonight was a good idea of Jan's.'

The restaurant was very busy. It was small and darkly lit with a trendy, minimalist décor. A jazz group was playing and a few people danced on a small dance-floor.

They were shown to a table at the far side of the room and a waiter brought them a menu each.

Kate found herself sitting opposite Nick again. She tried to concentrate on the menu but she was very conscious of Jan laughing with Andre. Somehow it seemed to highlight the silence between her and Nick.

She sneaked a glance at the other woman, watching her surreptitiously from behind the menu. Was Jan flirting with Andre? She glanced at Nick to see if he'd noticed. But he appeared to be engrossed in the menu.

When the waiter had taken their order, Andre suddenly turned to Kate and asked if she'd like to dance. Kate agreed and he pulled out her chair for her.

'So, have you ever been married Kate?' he asked her as they danced to a slow number, avoiding the other couples on the crowded floor.

'No, I haven't. What about you?' she asked, tipping her head back so that she could look up at him.

'Yes. I've been divorced for about a year now. I've got two children. A girl of six and a boy of four.'

'Do they live in Amsterdam?'

Andre shook his head. 'They live with their mother in Paris.'

'Do you see much of them?' Kate asked.

'Yes, as much as possible. They spend some weekends and most school holidays with me.'

Kate saw Nick and Jan get up and make their way hand

in hand to the dance-floor. She tried not to watch as they went into each other's arms.

'Jan told me that you and she used to date?' She forced her attention fully back on Andre.

'Yes…but at the time I was very cut up about my divorce. I don't think I was in a fit state to start dating again. Jan was very sympathetic… She's a great person.' He glanced over at the other couple. 'She seems very happy.'

'Yes, she does.' Kate was glad when the music changed and she could suggest that they sit down again.

The evening passed pleasantly enough after that, the conversation flowing very easily between the four of them. Jan was the life and soul of the party, becoming more gregarious and giggly with each course that was served.

Andre was right, she did seem very happy. Maybe Nick had already proposed, she thought suddenly.

As coffee was served the band played a very lively number and a lot of people got up to dance again.

'It's a bit energetic in here tonight, isn't it, Andre?' Jan asked. 'Do you remember the night we came in here and that folk musician was playing?'

Andre laughed. 'Music to hang yourself by?'

'That's the one.' She grinned at him. 'But you weren't in a particularly good frame of mind that night anyway.'

'No…how about a dance and I can redeem myself?' he asked.

Jan nodded and the two of them got up from the table and headed towards the dance-floor.

Nick glanced across at Kate. 'Shall we join them?' he asked quietly.

Somehow she managed a cool, almost indifferent smile. 'If you like,' she said. But it was purely an act because as she followed him from the table her senses were anything but cool.

She tried to keep her body slightly apart from his as he reached to take her into his arms, but it was impossible to keep a distance because the floor space was so tiny and packed with people. She was forced to move closer, and the feeling it conjured up inside her was a bittersweet ecstasy.

Kate remembered the last time she had danced with Nick at the wedding, remembered what had happened afterwards.

'Have you thought any further about coming to London next month?' Nick asked.

'Yes. I'm working in the morning so I'll just book my own flight.'

'Fair enough.' Nick nodded. 'So what do you think about Andre?'

'He seems a decent guy.'

'Have you asked him what star sign he is yet?'

'No.' Kate had to smile at that.

'You know, I read somewhere that finding a compatible star sign is much more complicated than you'd imagine. Apparently it depends on the time and place of birth.'

Something about the way he said that made her heart flip. She looked away from him again, confused, angry with herself for wanting something that could never be hers. 'You seem to be getting very interested in stargazing all of a sudden.'

'Maybe because I'm thinking of settling down. You need all the help you can get choosing the right partner, don't you think?' he asked playfully.

'I suppose you're right.' The music was changing and she took the opportunity to pull away from him. 'Thanks for the dance, Nick.'

Kate darted a glance over at their table. It was empty, Jan and Andre still out on the dance-floor, so she headed instead for the Ladies. She didn't want to be on her own with Nick. All this sudden talk about him settling down was making her very ill at ease. Surely he wasn't serious? Maybe it was his idea of a joke?

Jan followed her into the ladies' room a little while later as she stood at the mirror reapplying some lipstick.

'So what do you think?' Jan asked eagerly. 'It's been a really good evening, hasn't it?'

Kate smiled and tried to inflect some enthusiasm into her voice. 'Yes, and you were right about Andre—he is a very nice guy.'

Jan nodded. 'He's been through a rough time with his divorce but he seems to be getting over the worst of it now…don't you think?'

'He seems pretty together,' Kate agreed.

'Do you want to see him again?'

Kate shook her head. As much as she liked Andre, she didn't want to date him. Despite all that brave talk to Nick earlier, she really wasn't ready to get involved with anyone.

Jan nodded, then suddenly she put her hand on her arm. 'Kate, I need to tell you something,' she said urgently.

'What is it?' Kate swallowed down the feeling of dread and prepared herself to put on the act of her life if Jan told her that Nick had proposed.

Jan hesitated. 'But maybe I shouldn't say anything until I'm sure.'

Kate was reminded fiercely of the afternoon she had said something similar to Nick when she had thought Stephen was going to propose to her. 'Well, you can't leave me in suspense,' Kate said, curiosity tearing her apart. 'You've started now.'

'It's just that there is more behind tonight than I've told you… I haven't been completely honest.' Jan shifted from one foot to the other, looking embarrassed.

It was true, Kate thought, a cold chill of certainty racing through her as she waited for Jan to continue.

'I don't quite know how to say this…' Jan continued to waffle.

Did Jan guess that deep down she was in love with Nick? Was she dreading telling her that they were getting married because she knew it might hurt? 'I think I know what you're going to say,' Kate said, trying to soothe the situation, make things painless on them both.

'You do?' Jan looked at her in amazement.

'Well, reading a wedding magazine the other day was a bit of a give-away.' Kate smiled. 'You're in love with him, aren't you?'

'Is it that obvious?' Jan's eyes were like saucers. 'I mean, I've had my doubts myself…told myself that it would never work out between us. But, yes…you're right, I do love him. In all honesty, from the minute I first saw him I think I fell for him. I just can't get him out of my mind. Can't sleep at night, can't concentrate.'

'I can hear those wedding bells ringing already.' Kate grinned, a kind of crooked, brave, 'I might cry in a minute but I'm happy for you' grin. 'I'd better get my hat out and dust it down again.'

'Oh, thanks for being like this, Kate. You're a wonderful friend. But don't jump the gun too much; I've only got a feeling that he's ready to settle down, that we are going to work things out… I'm not a hundred per cent sure.'

'I think you'll work things out,' Kate said confidently and gave her friend a hug.

'So you really don't mind?' Jan asked cautiously.

'No, of course not,' Kate said emphatically, maybe too emphatically. 'What about London?' she asked suddenly. 'Are you going to go to the party?'

'The party?' Jan looked a bit blank for a moment.

'Nick's mum and dad's anniversary party.'

Jan bit down on her lip. 'Do you think he's expecting me to go? He never said he was.'

'Well, no…' Kate wanted to say, But I think you should, but she held back. 'Perhaps you should talk to Nick about it.'

Jan nodded. 'We'll have a long, long talk tonight. Sort everything out.'

The door opened and a few other women came in. Kate picked up her bag. 'Well, we'd better get back to the men,' she said swiftly. 'Otherwise they might just think that we've been talking about them.'

'And we'd never do that, would we?' Jan laughed.

The men were deep in conversation as they returned to the table.

Jan sat back down, but Kate didn't. She just wanted to go now; she had spent every last ounce of energy playing a part and she wasn't sure how long she could keep it up.

'Well, it's been a wonderful evening,' she said, glancing at her watch. 'But I suppose I'd better make a move.'

'I'll see you home,' Andre offered immediately, but before Kate could reply Jan jumped in.

'I thought we'd all go on to a club?' she suggested eagerly. 'I'm really in the mood for dancing the night away now.'

Kate shook her head and smiled. 'You go ahead and enjoy yourselves, but I really have to be going now. Do you think we can get the bill?' she asked, glancing over at Nick.

'The bill has already been settled,' he said.

She frowned.

'Don't start arguing, Katy, you know how it irritates me.' Nick smiled. 'There's a taxi rank around the corner—shall we walk to it?'

Much to Kate's dismay everyone agreed and got to their feet. She had hoped to make her escape quickly. Together they walked out into the cool of the evening.

The freshness of the air was a balm after the stuffy atmosphere.

'Sure you don't want to go to a club, Kate?' Jan asked hopefully as they walked along the quiet pavement.

'No, I really can't,' Kate murmured. She glanced at Nick; he was walking between Jan and herself and he was very quiet. Was he working out just what he would say to Jan when he got her back home? Maybe he was even hoping that she wouldn't really want to go to a club?

'I think we should call it a night, Jan,' he said. 'I've got to fly to Paris tomorrow.'

It started to rain suddenly. Large drops that came as a total surprise, bouncing off the pavements, drumming with cold, wet, icy fingers over them.

Kate was all right because she had her wrap to throw around her, but Jan was in a light summer dress and she shrieked in dismay as the deluge hit her.

They started to run towards the taxi rank, Andre putting a steadying hand on Kate's arm, Nick pulling Jan closer to him, protectively putting his jacket around her.

Kate thought about last night, how Nick had put his arm around her as they'd run through the rain. Suddenly she felt like crying.

There was only one taxi sitting at the rank. Kate's heart sank. Would this evening never end? she asked herself in despair.

They piled into the cab and Kate found herself wedged

next to Nick in the close, dark confines. She could feel his leg pressed close to hers and could hardly concentrate on the light-hearted conversation that flowed around her.

The taxi stopped outside Kate's apartment first.

Nick got out and reached to help her out of the car. 'Well, goodnight, everyone. Thanks for a lovely evening,' she said slightly breathlessly.

She ignored Nick's hand and stepped out onto the pavement unaided. 'Goodnight, Nick.' She didn't look at him, couldn't look at him.

CHAPTER ELEVEN

IT WAS strange how the love-bug could change a person, Kate thought as she sat at her desk the next day. You could be perfectly normal one moment, planning shopping lists and where to go at the weekend, and the next you were turned into this person who devoured wedding magazines and frantically tried to calculate how many bridesmaids would fit into a limousine and the cost of flower petals per ton. It was like some kind of illness.

Jan was very happy, though. Kate had never seen her so radiant; she positively shone. 'You were right, it's all worked out,' she hissed in an aside to Kate as they started the day's work. 'He proposed last night. We're planning a Christmas wedding.'

'I hope you'll be very happy, Jan,' Kate said quietly.

'Mum nearly fell over in shock when I phoned and told her this morning, and I think she was a bit disappointed that I don't want to go home to get married. But my life is here now.'

She started to go into detail about the wedding itself. She already knew where she wanted the function, and she'd seen a great dress in *Brides Destiny*.

Kate listened intently, and at the same time wished she were anywhere but here. 'Anyway, I'm going to have my sister as a bridesmaid and I wondered, Kate...if you would consider being my other bridesmaid?'

'Me?' Kate stared at her and just hoped she didn't look as horrified as she felt. She couldn't imagine anything worse than being a bridesmaid at Nick's wedding. It was a nightmare scenario. Quite frankly she was startled that Jan had even considered asking her. They hadn't known each other that long; Jan had only been with the company for six months.

'It would mean an awful lot to both of us,' Jan said. And suddenly Kate wondered if it had been Nick's idea.

The phone rang on Jan's desk. 'Just think about it, Kate,' she pleaded as she turned to answer it.

Luckily she was so overloaded with work that there wasn't time to think about it or talk about it again.

It was only when it was heading up to lunchtime, and Kate lifted her head from the manuscript that she was reading, that the subject came back to disturb her. In her mind's eye she saw herself walking down the aisle behind Jan. Nick standing waiting at the altar. She even saw him turning and smiling at Jan, flicking a quick, inquisitive glance over at her.

She couldn't do it…couldn't stand it!

'I'm going to go and choose my ring at lunchtime,' Jan murmured on her way past with a cup of coffee.

'Isn't Nick in Paris today?' Kate asked, puzzled.

'I think his flight is seven-thirty tonight.' Jan frowned. 'But I'm not sure.'

Kate was cycling home from work when the full magnitude of it all hit her.

Her horoscope had been right when it had said she was entering a period of profound change. Everything in her once well-ordered life seemed topsy-turvy. Nick was getting married. Stephen was…well, heaven alone knew where Stephen was.

At least she had been spared the indignity of having to give Jan an answer on the bridesmaid issue. Jan hadn't returned after lunch; she had requested the rest of the day off. Kate wondered if it was because Nick had asked her to accompany him to Paris tonight.

It was a grey day and it seemed to suit her mood perfectly. A misty rain slanted against her face as she turned the bicycle over the last bridge, past the café where she usually met Nick for coffee.

There were no tables and chairs outside today, and the windows of the café were steamed over so that the people inside were just dark silhouettes.

Kate put her head down, blinking the rain away from her eyes. By the time she got home, the rain seemed to have permeated through her fine clothing so that it clung damply to her skin, and she was freezing cold.

It was a relief to step through her front door. She stripped off her coat and left it dripping on a hook in the hall. Then started to divest herself of the rest of her clothing as she walked down to her bedroom. At least it was Friday, she told herself as she switched on her shower. She had a full weekend to relax and recover.

She'd had her shower and was drying her hair when the front doorbell rang. Her first instinct was to ignore it, but whoever it was was most insistent, leaning heavily on the bell.

Kate put on her dressing gown and went out to investigate.

She nearly fell over in shock when she opened the front door and found Nick standing on the doorstep.

Just looking at him set all her senses into chaos. Made a mockery of all those stern, sensible words she had been giving herself today—and, for that matter, all last night—about how she wasn't really in love with him anyway.

'Can I come in?' he asked as she kept him standing out in the rain.

'Sorry.' She stepped aside. 'I'm surprised to see you. I thought you'd be on your way to the airport now?'

'I am. I haven't got long.' His gaze moved over her slender figure, causing her to pull the white dressing gown a little closer around her body.

Nick reached into the inside pocket of his jacket and brought out some airline tickets. 'I just called to give you these.'

'What are they?' Kate looked at them cautiously.

'Tickets for a flight to London on the fifteenth, I took the liberty of booking them today.'

'But I—'

'I know what you said.' He stood up. 'But they are for late that afternoon. I thought even if you have to work in the morning, you'd make that.'

'Are you on that flight as well?'

'No. I'll be in Paris until then. But I'll fly direct from Charles-de-Gaulle into Heathrow. I'll arrive about the same time, so we can meet up and I'll be able to give you a lift into town.'

'OK…' She felt a sudden and unexpected lump in her throat. 'Thank you.'

'You mean it meets with your approval?' he asked wryly, watching as she put the tickets down on the hall table. 'You put up such a damn resistance to me organizing that flight that I half wondered if you'd throw the tickets at me.'

'I'm not going to throw the tickets at you.' She'd run out of energy to argue. She glanced towards the front door. 'Is Jan waiting for you in the car?'

Nick frowned. 'No.'

'I thought you were taking her to Paris?'

'What made you think that?'

'I just presumed.' She swallowed hard and forced herself to meet his eyes.

He was wearing a suit and he looked very businesslike, and very sexy. There was a part of her that wanted to reach out and unfasten his tie, ruffle his hair with her fingers and ask him to take her to bed.

The inclination appalled her. If Nick had been off limits before, he was definitely off the menu now.

'I suppose I should offer you my congratulations,' Kate said brightly. She forced herself to stand on tiptoe and kiss him on the cheek. It took a lot of will-power and a very strong resolve to ignore the signals from her body to stay that close, to wind her arms up and around his neck. 'You'll have to tell me what you want for a wedding present.'

'Do you want to tell me what you're talking about?' Nick placed a firm, detaining hand on her waist as she made to pull back from him.

'I'm talking about you and Jan getting married, of course.' She looked up into his eyes, her heart jumping fiercely in her chest. She could feel his hand burning through the fine silk of her dressing gown and she wanted him. She was ashamed of herself for being so weak, but she couldn't help it.

'What?'

He looked so stunned that she was taken aback. 'She told me—'

'I don't care what she told you. Jan and I are not getting married.' Nick cut across her decisively. 'In point of fact, we aren't even dating.'

Kate stared up at him as if he'd suddenly started to speak in a foreign language. 'But she said you asked her last night. You went shopping for a ring at lunchtime.'

Nick shook his head. 'No, I didn't.'

Kate pulled away from him. 'You mean you changed your mind?' Her first reaction was a wild exhilaration of relief, but then, when she remembered how happy Jan had been this morning, she felt equally distressed for her friend. 'Nick, how could you?'

'Quite easily, actually,' he said quietly, his eyes moving over her face, lingering on her lips.

She shivered slightly as he reached out and pulled her back firmly against him.

'So what happened?'

'What happened is, you've got it all wrong. Jan isn't getting married to me, she's getting married to Andre.'

Totally dazed by this, Kate could only stare at him, her mind flicking back over her conversation with Jan. 'But she told me that she was going to get married—'

'Yes, to Andre.'

Kate shook her head. 'I thought—'

'It's obvious what you thought. But you were wrong,' he said grimly.

Her eyes moved with tender concern over his face, as if searching for the truth. He did look a bit pale, she noticed, and tired, as if he hadn't slept very well last night. 'Oh, Nick! I'm so sorry.'

'Why?' Nick's eyes narrowed on her.

'Because I know you were serious about her—and I guess this is the first time a woman has finished with you,' Kate said with a shake of her head. 'It must come as a shock.'

'Are you trying to cheer me up?' Nick muttered dryly. 'Because you're not doing a very good job.'

'Sorry.' She pulled a face, and then caught the gleam of amusement in his dark eyes. At least he hadn't lost his sense of humour.

'Kate, I didn't love Jan,' he said gently. 'We went out

on a few dates and had a few chaste kisses, but that was as far as it went.'

'But you said last night that you'd decided to settle down—'

'Find the right woman,' he finished for her. 'That wasn't Jan.'

She looked up at him, her senses reeling.

'Jan told me last night that she was in love with Andre. She said planning a foursome gave her an excuse to call him up again without losing face.' Nick shrugged. 'And she knew that you were in no frame of mind for a serious date anyway.'

'That was true.' Kate met Nick's eye. 'Are you really OK?' she asked softly.

'I'm fine.' He tucked a stray strand of her hair behind her ear, his fingers feather-light against her skin as he looked into her eyes. 'But if you want to cheer me up,' he said suddenly, 'I won't object.'

She thought about his words, looked up at him, tipping her head to one side, regarding him contemplatively. Then she smiled, a teasing, slow smile that lit her eyes playfully. 'How do you propose I cheer you up?' she asked breathlessly.

He smiled and pulled her closer. Then bent his head and his lips found hers hungrily.

She responded unequivocally, her arms going up and around his neck, her body pressed close against his.

'I suppose we shouldn't be doing this,' he murmured.

'Because you might be on the rebound?' she murmured huskily, reaching to kiss him again.

'No, because I've got a flight to catch.'

'Catch a later one,' she said softly.

'Are you propositioning me, Kate Murray?'

She pulled back from him then. 'Yes,' she said softly, without any hint of reserve. 'I most certainly am.'

As she looked into the darkness of his eyes, she knew this was right. Yes, he was her friend and that friendship was very precious to her; she definitely didn't want to lose it. But stronger was the realization that she needed to give their relationship a chance to deepen, to develop into something stronger. Yes, it involved taking the risk of losing him as a friend, but maybe she had more to gain than to lose. And if she didn't take the plunge she might always wonder what might have been. Coming close to losing him had made her realize that.

He kissed her again, his kisses drugging, sensational, wildly passionate; they sent Kate's temperature soaring.

'I want you, Katy,' he said, his voice rasping against the tenderness of her skin now as his lips travelled over her eyes, her cheeks, down by her ears and her neck. 'I really want you.'

She stood on tiptoe, returning his caresses, her lips feverish against his.

Then she felt his hand hot against her skin as he pushed the dressing gown to one side.

Her body ached for him, but she forced herself to pull back. 'What are you going to do about your flight?' she asked him huskily.

'I'm going to forget about it,' he said with a growl, reaching to kiss her again.

Then he took her by the hand and led her very firmly towards the bedroom.

When Kate opened her eyes she was alone in the large double bed. She stretched lazily in the darkness, her mind filled with the drugging ecstasy of their lovemaking.

He had made love to her tenderly, slowly, provocatively

kissing and caressing her until she'd been helpless in his arms, held captive by a desire that had been so strong it had been overwhelming.

Even now, thinking about it brought the melting heat of longing flooding back again.

She glanced over at the illuminated clock next to her. It was almost midnight. She wondered where Nick was. He wouldn't have left without telling her, would he?

Sitting up, she flicked on the bedside lamp, and then reached for her dressing gown to go and investigate. She saw the light from the lounge spilling out into the darkened hall, and heard Nick's voice low and velvety in the silence of the apartment.

He was fully dressed, sitting on the arm of a chair, talking to someone on his mobile phone.

'If you could do that, it would be great,' he said softly. 'You're an angel.' He glanced up then and saw Kate standing silently watching him.

He smiled lazily at her, his eyes moving over her tenderly, in a way that made her body grow hot with desire.

'OK, speak to you later, Clare.' Nick put the phone down. 'Sorry, Kate, did I wake you? I was trying to be quiet.'

'You weren't going to leave without saying goodbye, were you?' she asked, her eyes narrowed on him.

'Of course not.' He got up from the chair and walked towards her, a purposeful light in his eyes that made her heart beat faster.

'Who is Clare?' she asked, trying not to be sidetracked by desire.

'Clare Aidan—she's the managing director of the company I'm dealing with at the moment. I think I told you about her.'

'Oh, yes. You had supper with her at a little restaurant

on the Left Bank in Paris,' she remembered and then frowned. 'It's nearly midnight, Nick. Isn't it a bit late to be phoning her?' she asked, trying not to sound suspicious.

He smiled. 'It's not midnight where Clare is. She's in America. I've got an appointment with one of her colleagues in Paris tomorrow morning, and I was phoning to see if she could reschedule it for me.' He reached out and pulled her into his arms. 'You see, I was full of good intentions of still making that meeting by catching a later flight. I got up, I got dressed and then I looked at you in that bed and I thought, I don't want to go to some stuffy meeting in Paris. I want to get back into bed with that gorgeous woman.'

He peppered the words with little kisses. Kate smiled and wound her arms up and around his neck. 'It's nice to know I'm such a good influence on you,' she murmured, kissing him back.

'What's this Clare like, anyway?' she asked, unfastening his tie and starting to unbutton his shirt.

'She's about fifty, very nice—'

'Is she attractive?' Kate's hand lingered by the fastening of Nick's belt.

'Yes, she is. But not as attractive as you.'

Kate laughed. 'Well, you would say that, wouldn't you?' she teased. 'Because I'm the woman who is going to make mad, passionate love to you and make you forget what line of business you are even in.'

'I've already forgotten,' Nick assured her. Then, taking her completely by surprise, he swept her up off her feet and carried her back to the bedroom.

'This reminds me of the night we spent together at that hotel,' Kate said breathlessly as he placed her down on the bed.

'One of the best nights of my life,' Nick said seriously.

'Was it?' For a moment she held the darkness of his eyes. 'I was so worried afterwards. I thought that we'd destroyed our friendship.'

'I must admit I worried about it myself.' Nick shook his head. 'There have been lots of times when I wanted to just take you in my arms and kiss you until you were senseless. Then I'd pull back, telling myself that what we had was too precious to risk losing. But we'll always be friends, Katy, no matter what. I love you too much to ever let you go out of my life.'

Kate swallowed hard. She gently touched his face. 'What did you just say?' she asked tremulously, hardly daring to believe what she had heard.

'I said I love you. I think I always have, I just didn't realize how much until you told me that you were thinking of marrying Stephen and it hit me out of nowhere.'

He kissed her, cradling her close to his body. 'I know Stephen hurt you badly, Kate. I know you still aren't over all of that—'

'But I am over Stephen,' she cut in fiercely. 'Nick, I love you.' Kate pulled away from him and held his eyes earnestly. 'I love you with all my heart. Like you, I just didn't realize what you meant to me… It was staring me in the face all the time and yet I just didn't see it. Not until I started to really think about spending the rest of my life with Stephen did the truth start to dawn on me.'

'And you're not still in love with him?' He sounded incredulous.

She shook her head. 'Stephen did me the biggest favour when he left. I care about him…but I don't love him.'

'His bag is still sitting in your hall cupboard, you know,' he said roughly.

'Is it?' She smiled and shook her head. 'He must have

forgotten it when he took the rest of his stuff. I'll throw it out if—'

Nick kissed her before she could finish the sentence and then she forgot what she was saying anyway, as once more they were lost in passion.

The shrill sound of the alarm clock woke Kate. For a moment she didn't know what day it was, or where she was. She felt disorientated. She didn't remember setting the alarm clock—was it a workday?

She blinked in the bright sunshine that flooded across the bedroom and blindly turned off the alarm. There was a piece of paper leaning against it. She struggled to sit up, and as she did memories of last night came racing back. She smiled as she read the piece of paper.

Gone home to get showered and changed.
Meet you at the café at ten for breakfast.
Love Nick.
PS, don't be late.

Kate smiled and leaned back against the pillows. I'm in love, she thought dreamily, remembering Nick's kisses, his body pressed close to hers. She turned her head to look at the time and then with a shriek leapt out of bed.

It was nine-fifteen. She hadn't time to dream, she had to hurry and get showered.

The day was crisp and fresh, with a clear blue sky. It was as if the rain of the last few days had washed everything down.

Kate cycled over the last of the bridges and looked over towards the café. All the tables and chairs were out, but there weren't many people. She could see Nick waiting for her; he was standing on the perimeter of the café leaning on the rails above the canal. He looked relaxed and handsome in the bright sunlight.

'Good morning.' He turned as she approached. She felt her heart drumming against her chest as he reached to kiss her. But, unlike other times when they had met, this time his kiss was warm and passionately on the lips.

'Morning.' She pulled back from him, feeling suddenly shy.

'How are you this morning?' he asked gently, his eyes moving over her face, and then the curves of her figure. She was wearing a pale blue trouser suit that was casual and yet very stylish.

'I don't know.' She laughed. 'Tired, I think. Someone kept me up late last night.'

'Someone with exquisite taste.' Nick kissed her again. 'We'll have breakfast in a minute, but first I want you to help me with some shopping.'

'What kind of shopping?' Kate asked in surprise.

'I want to buy a ruby pendant for my mother's anniversary. There's a jeweller's around the corner.' He took hold of her hand. 'I just need your opinion on something.'

They strolled hand in hand to the jeweller's window. Kate peered in at the rows of gleaming gemstones. 'Which one do you like?'

'Actually, it's this window I want you to look in.' Nick tugged at her hand and led her further down.

She was faced with row upon row of diamond rings.

'This is one of the good points about living in Amsterdam,' he said as she looked up at him in surprise. 'There's a good choice of engagement rings.'

'I don't know what to say,' Kate murmured, overcome with astonishment.

'Just say yes,' Nick said, looking deeply into her eyes. 'I love you, Kate, and I want you for my wife.'

For a second his face blurred as tears distorted her vision.

Then he took her into his arms, holding her tightly against him. 'So what do you say?' he asked.

'I say, yes.' She smiled, reaching up to kiss him.

It was a while before they broke apart.

'And this afternoon we can take another look at that house,' Nick said gently, stroking her hair back from her face.

'The one you are thinking of turning into apartments?' she asked shakily.

'No, the one I'm thinking of turning into a family home for the woman I love,' he said quietly.

The world's bestselling romance series.

HARLEQUIN®
Presents

Seduction and Passion Guaranteed!

**Harlequin Presents®
invites you to escape into
the exclusive world of royalty
with our royally themed books**

By Royal Command

Look out for:
The Prince's Pleasure
by **Robyn Donald**, #2274
On sale September 2002

**Pick up a Harlequin Presents® novel
and you will enter a world of
spine-tingling passion and
provocative, tantalizing romance!**

Available wherever Harlequin books are sold.

International bestselling author

SANDRA MARTON

invites you to attend the

WEDDING *of the* YEAR

Glitz and glamour prevail in this volume
containing a trio of stories in which
three couples meet at a
high society wedding—and
soon find themselves
walking down the aisle!

Look for it in November 2002.

HARLEQUIN®
*M*akes any time special®

Restore the healthy balance to your life in a guilt-free way.

———————— ❦ ————————

QUIET MOMENTS

This month, the Harlequin Presents® series offers you a chance to pamper yourself!

Enjoy a FREE Bath Spa Kit with only four proofs of purchase from September 2002 Harlequin Presents novels. Special Limited-Time Offer.

Offer expires November 29, 2002.

YES! Please send me my FREE Quiet Moments Bath Spa Kit without cost or obligation, except for shipping and handling. Enclosed are four proofs of purchase (purchase receipts) from September Harlequin Presents novels and $3.50 shipping and handling fee, in check or money order, made payable to Harlequin Enterprises Ltd.

598 KJN DNDF

Name (PLEASE PRINT)

Address   Apt. #

City   State/Prov.   Zip/Postal Code

IN U.S., mail to:	IN CANADA, mail to:
Harlequin Presents Bath Kit Offer	Harlequin Presents Bath Kit Offer
3010 Walden Ave.	P.O. Box 608
P.O. Box 9023	Fort Erie, Ontario
Buffalo, NY 14269-9023	L2A 5X3

FREE SPA KIT OFFER TERMS
To receive your free Quiet Moments Bath Spa Kit, complete the above order form. Mail it to us with four proofs of purchase (your purchase receipts). Requests must be received no later than November 29, 2002. Your Quiet Moments Bath Kit costs you only $3.50 for shipping and handling. The free Bath Spa Kit has a retail value of $16.99 U.S./$24.99 CAN. All orders subject to approval. Products in kit illustrated are for illustrative purposes only and items may vary (retail value of items always as previously indicated). **Please allow 6-8 weeks for delivery. Offer good in Canada and the U.S. only. Offer good only while supplies last. Offer limited to one per household.**
© 2002 Harlequin Enterprises Limited

Visit us at www.eHarlequin.com   HPPOP07